MW00892287

Evolution's Angels

By Nick Iuppa

This book is a work of fiction.

Names, characters, places, and incidents are either the product of the author's imagination or are used fictitiously. Any resemblance to actual persons, living or dead, or to actual events or locales is entirely coincidental.

Evolution's Angels (Formerly published as Species II)

Copyright © 2023 by Nick Iuppa. All rights reserved, including the right to reproduce this book, or portions thereof, in any form. No part of this text may be reproduced, transmitted, downloaded, decompiled, reverse engineered, or stored in or introduced into any information storage and retrieval system, in any form or by any means, whether electronic or mechanical, without the express written permission of the author. The scanning, uploading, and distribution of this book via the Internet or via any other means without the permission of the publisher is illegal and punishable by law. The publisher does not have any control over and does not assume any responsibility for author or third-party websites or their content.

Cover image Copyright:
ISBN: 9798335775878
Published BY Dos Milagros Press
Visit the author's website @ www.nickiuppa.com

For Dr. Nicholas V. Iuppa, my Dad, who always
loved science and a good story.

A new species is a type of plant or animal that has developed unique characteristics and separated from other members of its species....

New species can form through genetic divergence, reproductive isolation, or gradual changes in an entire lineage in response to environmental changes.

- Google AI Overview

Suppose there is a little girl out there, somewhere today... this morning!... who has within her, lying dormant at present... the power someday to crack the very planet in two like a China plate in a shooting gallery?

Stephen King – FIRESTARTER

TABLE OF CONTENTS

The Characters

Rochester, New York
Melissa (Missy) Washington – inner-city teenager
Serena Washington – Melissa's mother
Javon Washington – Melissa's brother
Dr. Richard (Rick) Michael – Melissa's ER doctor
Tracy Moore – ER nurse

Hollywood, CA
Brad Dockster – Newstalk radio shock jock
Allan Allgood – Brad's pen name when he writes for the
Los Angeles Chronicle
Debbie Dockster – Brad's wife
Alex – their baby son
Ed Feeney – editor-in-chief of the Los Angeles Chronicle
– hires Dockster to write editorials

Washington, DC
Bobbie Jenkins – Homeland Security – Special Agent
Niles Powers – Homeland Security agent – reports to
Bobbie
Sonny Grabowski – Undercover agent with motorcycle
gang
Chopper City – Lost Mountain, Utah
Josh Purdy – the King of Chopper City, motorcycle gang
leader – head of anti- New Species movement called
Humanity First
Emma Minson – Purdy's administrative assistant and
"Best Crack Shot in Saint Louis County"
Donny Minson – her husband

In Sam's Romance Novel
Parker Ashley – new office worker in midtown Manhattan
Jason Preston – midtown manager and heartthrob

Aswidth State University Students in Aswidth, Texas
Police Captain facing protesters.
Andy Rechsteiner
Protesters
Joanie Ridgeway
Tim Morgan
Charlie Manual
Andrea Rodrigues
UC – Berkeley
Carter Woodley
Harold Tryon
Chang-Chang Woo

Prologue

Kaitlin Wolf pushed open the clear glass door to the office and slipped inside. The moon shining through the back window barely provided any light as she made her way to the desk in the far corner of the room. She sat in the ergonomically perfect chair and looked up at the massive desktop computer.

Barely able to see the keyboard in the darkness, she still was able to punch in the password the doctor had given her, and the screen flashed to life. Its background wallpaper showed a dazzling nighttime view of New York's Times Square.

On top of the scene sat a confusing jumble of folders, each with a crazy name and a tiny image. It seemed quite unlike the fastidious old man who used the computer, Kaitlin thought.

Still, she quickly spotted what she was looking for...almost in the center of the screen, a folder with the image of a cartoon pair of powder-blue jeans-shorts named *PinkyBleue.* She recognized it as the code name for the folder containing the manuscript for the professor's latest steamy romance novel.

Kaitlin opened it, selected the document at the top of the list, and set to work.

Over the next hour and a half, she read and edited three new chapters about a young woman who took a train from Duluth to New York to learn about life and love in the big city. Of course, gentlemen on the train were pleased to make her acquaintance and give her—perhaps—an overly encouraging view of her life to come.

"Who reads this drivel," Kaitlin asked herself. But she knew. There was a shelf full of the Professor's New York Times Bestselling romance novels on a bookcase beside the desk.

The people who bought them wanted happy endings to help them feel that everything would work out in the end. Who could blame them? Kaitlin thought

2

as she renamed, saved, and closed the edited version of the document. Life in the real world was tough enough.

After a moment, despite the jumble of images on the screen, she now saw her reflection looking back at her...illuminated only by moonlight...a college sophomore with straight black hair, dark eyes, and a welcoming smile.

"I'm pretty," she thought as she brushed her hair back from her forehead, yawned, and was about to leave when... "Hey, what's this?" she asked as she refocused on a folder just to the right of *PinkyBleue.*

"CutePuppies."

"WTF?" Kaitlin murmured, shaking her head.

The professor's security system obviously involved giving unusual names to his folders...names completely unrelated to their content. "Silly old man," the girl said fondly, and with sophomoric confidence, she opened the folder.

She saw a long list of reports—almost one every few days for what looked like a solid year.

She opened the first document and began to read.

Kaitlin Wolf was still reading as dawn gently awakened the campus.

"They'll be coming in soon; better go," she told herself. But before she did, she slipped a thumb drive into the computer's USB port and dragged the folder onto it.

"Interesting stuff," she murmured as she shut down the computer, leaving a well-edited manuscript and a folder full of startling reports that Kaitlin now brought home with her. She knew she shouldn't talk about them to anyone, of course...it was just too *amazing* and not at all what she was hired to work on.

Still...

PART ONE
ABOMINATIONS

ONE—LILLIE
(Felicity, California—Northern Sierra Foothills)

1

Adam Allonzo moved to the hospital bed and took his daughter's tiny hand. It was so cold...despite the blankets, the scorching heat outside, and the burns on the little girl's entire left arm where the wildfire had attacked her.

He raised her fingers to his lips and kissed them. But Lillie didn't move.

"She's still unconscious," the nurse whispered as she glanced at the bank of monitors attached to the child's body. "But she's doing as well as she can."

Adam closed his eyes, squeezed the tears away, and nodded. "Will she be all right?"

"Of course," said the nurse, who was a short, sweet-faced Filipino woman dressed in grey-green scrubs and sensible shoes. "Her body just needs time to recover from the shock."

"And the burns," added Lillie's mom. The girl's left arm was wrapped in bandages. The burns were certainly painful but, thankfully, confined to that one area.

Donna Allonzo looked at her husband. They searched each other's eyes for a moment...and in that instant, they shared a memory that terrified them both.

A raging fire drawing nearer to their home in Felicity, California...in the foothills of the Sierra Nevada mountains.

Adam's determination to stay and fight the fire while his wife drove herself and their little girl to safety.

"Get in the car, Adam! We're not going without you," Donna shouted.

"I'm staying here!" And he grabbed the garden hose and trained it on the edge of their property.

"I can save the house...I know I can."

Then, four-year-old Lillie jumped from their car and rushed toward her sandbox. She grabbed her little pail, scooped up water from a puddle in the grass, and ran directly at the wall of flames. She threw the tiny bucketful of water at the raging fire.

"I'm going to help you, Daddy!" she shouted, and then, despite the searing heat, she turned and smiled back at her dad just as the old tree on the edge of the property exploded into flames. A small branch split from the tree and jumped toward the little girl, grazing her in the temple and knocking her down as the fire surged forward and caught the sleeve of her shirt. Fortunately, Adam was beside her by then. He grabbed her, threw her to the ground, and pressed her burning arm against the still-dry earth, suffocating the flames. But the damage was done.

"Oh, Daddy, it hurts so bad!" Lillie sobbed as he carried her to the waiting car. He pressed her into Donna's arms, raced to the driver's side, threw himself into the seat, turned the ignition, and sped away.

In his rear-view mirror, Adam could see the wildfire breaching the yard's perimeter, jumping onto the roof of the neighboring house, and beginning to engulf it. The last thing he saw was more flames flying toward the top of their home...the new addition they'd just added...the kitchen Donna had dreamed of for so long.

"Mommy...Daddy! It hurts so bad," Lillie murmured.

"I know, sweetheart," Donna whispered as she held her little girl. She had wrapped Lillie's arm in wet bandages fashioned out of torn strips of her own clothing and soaked with bottled water.

"We'll be at the hospital soon. They'll make the hurt go away."

She looked down at Lillie's face, now twisted in pain, a bruise rising where the branch struck her—no blood, just a bruise—then the girl's body went limp, and she was unconscious.

2

Dr. Paul Grinnell entered the emergency room, where Lillie lay sleeping.

"I think an MRI is in order," he said with a stoic expression.

"What do you mean?" asked Donna. "Why?"

"There's significant bruising where that falling branch hit her head. We just want to make sure there's no additional damage."

"Damage???"

"Just a precaution," said Grinnell in his most comforting tone. "We want to be safe, rule out any negative possibilities."

Donna glanced at her husband and then shook her head.

"It's okay, Mommy," murmured the little girl.

The conversation with the doctor had drawn her parents' attention away from Lillie. So, no one noticed when her eyes suddenly popped open. But now, everyone turned toward her, and the little girl managed a weak smile.

"Lillie! Are you all right?"

"I...I think so, Mommy."

Everyone rushed to her bedside. Dr. Paul glanced up at the monitors and studied them. "Thank God," he whispered.

"Whatever the doctor wants to do," Lillie said, "you should let him."

Dr. Paul glanced at the girl's parents, amazed that Lillie could be so clear-thinking after the trauma of the burns and the blow to her head.

"Remarkable child," he said. "Are you in pain, sweetheart?"

"A little, but it's okay. Is my daddy all right?"

Adam sat in a chair in the corner of the room. Studying his daughter, his eyes burning with guilt.

"I should have taken you to safety as soon as they warned us," he said.

"It's okay, Daddy. You were trying your best. I love you…Mommy, too."

"Let's do that MRI, get it over with," said Dr. Paul. "We'll all feel better when we have it behind us, and Lillie can go home again."

"I'd like that," said the little girl. "But will it hurt?"

Donna put her hand on Lillie's shoulder and turned defensively toward the doctor. "We don't want to put her through any more suffering."

"It's important," said Dr. Paul, "for her own good." And then, turning to Lillie, he added, "And the MRI won't hurt, Honey. It might feel a little confining—a little tight—but otherwise…."

"Tight is okay," said Lillie with a weak smile.

"Good," said the doctor. "So, let's make it happen."

@@

Two hours later, Dr. Paul studied the results of the MRI. "No trauma...no injury. Looks very good," he said. "Only..."

"I've never seen anything like that," added the technician who stood beside him. "It must be some kind of physical anomaly?"

"I guess we can call it that," answered Dr. Paul, a knowing expression touching his face.

3

"The test results are just fine," said the doctor when he returned to Lillie's room to face her parents. "We'd like to treat your daughter's burns for one more day and then release her."

"So, there is no damage from the blow to her head?" asked Adam.

"The area looks normal. There's a minor aberration but nothing to be concerned about."

"What do you mean?"

"It seems to be nothing more than a natural anomaly. It won't affect her, I'm sure. Some people are born with six toes. It's something like that. So, we'll just note it, but you don't need to worry about it. Just get Lillie back on her feet, and then you can try to return to your normal lives."

Of course, Dr. Paul Grinnell did more than note the unusual physiology of Lillie's brain. He sent a full report and images from the MRI to Leland University, where his good friend and colleague, Dr. Kathleen Kelly, was starting to notice an emerging pattern.

4

The drive back to Felicity the next day was one of the most depressing rides Adam Allonzo had ever taken. It all seemed so horrific, even if he didn't think of little

Lillie, her burns, and the pain she'd had to endure, even if he didn't think of his last sight of their home as flames leaped from the neighbor's roof to theirs.

To clear his head, he turned on the radio. It was set to his favorite news/talk station, and shock jock Brad Dockster—who was good for a distracting rant on any topic—was just starting his morning broadcast.

"YES, FRIENDS," he began with all the fervor of a Sunday morning fire and brimstone preacher,

> *Time for another edition of **THAT'S WHAT I THINK** from your friend, Brad Dockster, who ALWAYS tells it like it is.*
> *TODAY'S*
> *TOPIC...CALAMITIES!*
> *Because I see a whole host of disasters, economic catastrophes, wars, and other nastiness lurking around the corner.*
> *For example, what do people in California do as these wildfires get wilder, their reservoirs get drier, and*

there are no longer any crops in the fields?

I'll tell you! First, as these wildfires continue, a bunch of desperate Californians burn up like raw kindling on a windy night. And then the rest of 'em STARVE: no food coming from the most fertile valley in the world. It's all burnt up, friends. And no food means no work, no life in the big city, and no tech.

Earthquakes! Fire and brimstone! I tell you, friends, let's face it. California is going to die...just before it slides into the sea.

No significant loss, you say. I'd like to agree with you, except I'm sure it will take the rest of the country—and our economy AND ALL OUR JOBS—with it.

So where do we turn next for sustenance? You ask.

China and Russia, that's where. And when that happens, friends, America falls into second and then third-rate oblivion.

Our food, our jobs, our schools, and our whole way of life...all gone because the people in California can't control their wildfires. All they have to do is rake up the leaves and needles that fall under the trees every year. But of course, they don't...THE LAZY LUGS! (Pardon my French.) They're too busy blaming it all on the president.

Anyway, you heard it here first, friends, cause THAT'S WHAT I THINK.

And now a word from tasty-nut peanut butter.

"Good lord," said Donna. "Why do you listen to that man?"

"Don't really know anymore," Adam answered as he turned off the radio. "He was popular during the election...really loved calling out the hypocrites in Washington. But now that the election is over, it seems the guy doesn't know what to talk about. So, he just looks for doom and gloom wherever he can find it. He probably just enjoys scaring us."

Donna shrugged. "Fear is power, I guess?"

"Must be," said Adam as he turned his attention back to the road.

The broad highway now wound through a haunted landscape filled with the charred remains of towering pine trees, their trunks burned black, their branches broken and bare of needles. Each bend in the road offered new vistas crowded with the dismal statuary of the naked forest. Corpses of fallen tree trunks lay broken amid the skeletal shapes still standing, the earth no longer verdant but bare of underbrush and painted dirty grey by the ash from the fires.

"I don't like this, Daddy," Lillie sighed. "I don't want to live in a world like this. We need to fix it."

"I wish we could," Adam answered. "I'm just not sure we can, sweetheart, even if we knew how."

Lillie's eyes brightened with a look of determination. "Of course, we *can*, Daddy," she said. "I know we can." But at that sorrowful moment, Adam wasn't sure her word "we" included his generation.

"Maybe someday," was all he could answer.

They took the same turn-off and drove through the narrow streets of Felicity, seeing five homes burned to the ground for every one even partially standing. Nothing had escaped the ravages of the wildfire.

"Brace yourselves," Adam said as he slowly wheeled onto the street that led to their subdivision.

"I can't look," Donna sighed and closed her eyes.

20

"There's no way we can start over," Adam said. "We just don't have the funds. Maybe for a few repairs, some minor fixes...only..."

"YAY!" Lillie suddenly interrupted. "LOOK, MOMMY, OUR HOUSE IS OKAY!"

"Mostly," Adam added. And Donna opened her eyes to see they were parked in their own driveway. Even though three nearby homes had been destroyed and their new addition looked severely damaged, most of their home was intact.

"We can fix it, Mommy," Lillie added. "We really can."

TWO—ÁNGEL
(Outside Tucson, Arizona)

1

Talley Antone sat as still as she could. She needed to fidget, and Antonio said that would be all right, but he would be done soon, and the little girl would do anything to help him finish the painting, even sit so still every pore in her body itched. After all, this was the painting that would hang at the entryway to the tribe's casino, helping all the patrons know that the profits from gambling would benefit this little girl and her school.

Across the room, the old painter dabbed away with his brushes, always with that crooked smile, satisfied with his work, never unhappy, never worried, never thinking of anything else when creating a portrait.

22

Talley's grandfather, the tribal chief, had agreed to the portrait. So had her father and mother. She would be a worthy representative of the tribe and her school, someone who would get the patrons to open their hearts and their wallets and gamble freely to help support the kids of the reservation.

Antonio Rivera—the old artist—stepped back from his work, rolling the brush between his fingertips, studied the painting for a moment more, cocked his head, and then stepped forward. He dabbed at the canvas one last time and finally proclaimed, "I'm done...it's finished." And with a sweeping motion of his arm, he added, "Come see."

Talley jumped down from the stool and ran across the room, beads rattling native dress whooshing as she came. Then she stopped, stepped behind the artist and his painting, and...

"Oh, my God!" she gasped. Tears filled her eyes. "It is so...so... Am I really that pretty?"

"You are, Talley," Antonio whispered, now feeling his own tears spill down his cheeks. "Far more beautiful than anything I could ever portray. I only hope that..."

But before the old man could finish, Talley rushed to the door and called out, "Mama! You have to see this. Come quick!"

And with more than a little commotion, Talley's heavy-set Mama rushed into the room, heading immediately to the front of the painting and looking at it.

"Oh, yes," she sighed. "You've captured Talley perfectly."

She began to cry...not gently like the artist and his model, but with a tremendous explosion of tears.

Finally, Mama said, "Wrap it up, Antonio. We'll take it with us."

The artist turned to the two women and gave them a smile of gratitude as though they were the ones who had worked magic.

"But let me keep it overnight," he said. "Please. I'll get it framed for you and deliver it myself. I want the paint to dry before anyone handles it. And..." he added with a knowing smile, "I want to sit with it for one evening...share its company."

"We don't want to trouble you, Antonio," Mama said. "You have so much to do here at the ranch. You were kind enough to paint this portrait for us. We couldn't think of..."

"I insist," the artist said firmly.

He knew he had a cattle ranch to run, a great sprawling enterprise out in the Arizona desert. It was now so threatened by the growing heat that he couldn't stop worrying about it, imagining every possible kind of disaster that could befall his family and their business.

Better to enjoy this simple work...something he did all by himself. Painting Talley's portrait had been such a great distraction, the happiest he had been in years.

"And I'd like Ángel to see it," he added.

At the mention of Antonio's twelve-year-old grandson, Mama's expression changed.

"Oh, yes, Ángel. Of course. We'd like him to see the painting too, wouldn't we, Talley?"

Talley frowned and crossed her arms. She had pictured herself presenting the portrait to her grandfather later this same evening. She really didn't want to wait.

"I guess," she sighed reluctantly, as she began to chew on the corner of her lip.

Antonio understood. In fact, he found her eagerness flattering.

"Please, little Talley," he said. "Let the painting stay with me for just one night...let the paint dry, for heaven's sake. And let me show her to Ángel. Then she'll belong to you and your people forever."

Under the stern glare of her mother, the girl sighed and nodded in agreement.

2

26

Ángel stared at the painting, his smile growing wider. "How did you ever end up on a ranch, Papa?" he asked. "You should be a portrait painter, or…"

"An animator for the Walt Disney Studio," Antonio said with a nostalgic grin. "That's what I wanted to be— what I studied for. But, you know, one does what one has to do. After all, the ranch has been in our family for five generations."

"Sure," said Ángel. He understood more completely than his widowed grandfather would ever know. Just as Papa had taken him in after Ángel's father, mother, and older sister had died in a plane crash coming back from an Ill-fated college visit, just as little Ángel had given up that comfortable home and family in Los Angeles to live in the Arizona desert with his grandfather. "We do what we have to do."

The boy stepped closer to the painting. "The love in Talley's eyes is perfect," he said. "She's looking out at everyone and blessing them."

The old man shrugged. How could a kid—not even a teenager—recognize something like that, let alone explain it? It wasn't the first of Ángel's surprising observations. And there would be more, Antonio was sure of it. He could only marvel.

And—speaking of eyes—the boy's eyes glowed with a silvery fascination that had unnerved the old man from time to time. Still, he loved Ángel dearly.

"Want to ride fences with me tomorrow?" Antonio asked. It was mostly a symbolic act. He had a steady cadre of men who did the day-to-day work. But this was really another way for the old man to get away from the ledgers and financial worries that so consumed him these days. And it allowed him to assess the state of the property he inherited from his grandfather.

Ángel's eyes brightened with that silvery glow. Papa only offered to share the experience with him on rare occasions, usually when he was especially pleased. "Just because I liked his painting?" the boy asked himself. But out loud, he simply said, "Awesome."

28

3

The following morning, the old man and the boy saddled up by 8:00 AM and rode their horses slowly along the edge of the fence, inspecting for broken wire and finding none. At this point, Antonio was a little ahead of the boy when he suddenly spotted a sprawling hulk low in the arroyo and urged his horse forward.

"Mother of God!" the old man sighed as he dismounted. It was a dead cow rotting in the dried-out bed of the river. Its stomach and throat had been torn open and eaten by coyotes. Its skin had baked onto its bones, eyes eaten, lips torn away, teeth forming an unholy grin that seemed to say, "I haven't had a drink in weeks. What did you expect?"

Ángel rode slowly up to his grandfather, stood in the saddle, took in the gruesome sight, and nodded sadly.

"Tough," he murmured.

"More than that," said Antonio pointing beyond the sunbaked carcass. "See there. The river is already bone dry, and we're only partway through June. The whole place has gone dead...and it's burning up."

He took a kerchief and wiped the sweat from his face. "What the hell's happening?"

"No wonder the cattle are dying," said the boy.

"Our property's just too damn low," said his grandfather. "Only two thousand feet of altitude. Most of the other ranches are at higher elevations. The King Ranch sits at four thousand feet, not as susceptible to the drought. But we're stuck down here where Grandpa staked his claim long before the heat became so merciless."

"What about our other springs?" Ángel asked, trying to add a sense of hope.

"They're all the same," Antonio answered. "They used to go dry in August, but now, the water's gone as early as June, and it doesn't return until November."

"At least you've got the wells," the boy said, "the ones great grandad dug."

"Yeah," Antonio said, taking one last look at the dead cow, then turning his horse and moving along the fence. "For now, but who knows how long they'll last? Groundwater's going. The quality of the beef is deteriorating. We'll have to cut back on the size of the herd."

Antonio came to a slight rise in the land and suddenly picked up the pace, moving more quickly along the fence line, barely looking at the fences anymore...just trying to get out of the burning sun. Then, when he came to the shade of a broad tree, he stopped and turned to Ángel. The old man's expression was grim.

"Might have to sell. That's what I'm thinking."

"You can't do that," Ángel said almost automatically.

"Might have to...if I can find a buyer. But, let's face it, who would want this God-forsaken place now?"

Ángel nodded sadly and began trying to guide his mount closer to his grandfather when suddenly the horse jumped sideways. She struggled with her footing and went down on her side, landing on Ángel's hip and slamming his head against a nearby rock.

"Rattler," growled Antonio as he dismounted, seeing the snake winding away from them. Ángel's horse had righted herself by then, but the boy still lay on the ground, barely conscious.

Antonio felt the urge to pull him to his feet, throw him onto the horse, and rush him back to the ranch. But instead, he pulled out his cell phone.

"Jack!" he called to his foreman. "Ángel's horse got spooked by a rattlesnake. He's taken a nasty fall. Someone has to get the old Jeep up here and fast. We're at the big pine on the ridgetop.

"Bring a stretcher too. We'll have to get him to the hospital... take x-rays of everything: his hip, chest, and head.

"That's right...hit it against a rock. He's still pretty woozy.

"Dios Mio, I hope he doesn't die. God! Don't let that happen."

THREE—MELISSA
(Rochester, New York)

1

Tracy Moore wheeled the gurney from the ambulance into the Emergency Room of Strong Memorial Hospital. She was almost running, shouting loudly as soon as she entered the automated doors.

"TEENAGER...FEMALE...MULTIPLE GUNSHOT WOUNDS TO THE HEAD AND BODY...EXTREME BLOOD LOSS!"

"WAIT! LET ME SEE. LET ME SEE MY MELISSA!" shouted a young woman running behind Tracy. She seemed hardly older than the victim and yet had to be the girl's mother.

Tracy stopped and turned. "YOU HAVE TO WAIT HERE!" she said forcefully.

"But I need to be with my baby."

"No...you don't. WAIT HERE. We don't have time for this."

A young teenage boy ran up to the frantic woman, put his arms around her, and pulled her back from the entryway.

"It's okay, Mom," he said. "Let her go. We'll stay here and pray."

The woman let the boy pull her back and watched as Tracy pushed the gurney into the enclosed alcove within the ER.

"We're praying for you, Melissa," the mother called. "Jesus will bless you, Honey."

Immediately inside the emergency room, Dr. Rick Michael helped Tracy and another orderly transfer Melissa to an examining table, quickly removing the compression bandages placed on the girl's chest and forehead in the ambulance.

"Nasty stuff," he murmured. "Come on, help me roll her over...

"Checking for exit wounds now."

34

The orderlies turned Melissa onto her side. She was still unconscious.

"Damn," the doc said as he ran his fingers over the girl's back. "No exit wound."

He moved his hand to her scalp, running his fingers through her blood-caked hair, and added, "Can't feel an exit wound from the bullet she took to the head either.

"They're still in her."

Rick looked across at Tracy, who was no stranger to street shootings. She shook her head and closed her eyes for a moment.

"Let's get an MRI of the chest and head area right now," Rick said.

José pulled up another gurney, helped Tracy and the doctor lift Melissa onto it, and then rushed the girl to Imaging.

By then, the girl's mother had calmed enough to provide the necessary insurance and identification to the Medical Center. Melissa was thirteen-year-old Melissa (Missy) Washington of West Main Street,

Rochester, New York. Her brother, Javon, was eleven. Mom, Serena, was twenty-nine.

2

Five hours later, Dr. Rick Michael entered the ER waiting room. Serena sat there; her head bent in prayer. Javon was beside her, barely able to concentrate on the video game he was trying to play on his phone.

"Mrs. Washington," the doctor began as he approached the woman. He noted that she was slim, intelligent looking, dressed neatly in an inexpensive short sleeve dress of yellow cotton. It came to her knees, and the neckline was high and modest.

When Serena saw the doctor, there was a hint of that possessive panic that Nurse Tracy had witnessed. But the young woman had calmed significantly. Perhaps partly from the hours spent in that small waiting room and partly from growing exhaustion.

"How is she, Doctor?" Serena asked.

"She's conscious," he answered with a smile of relief.

"Thank the Lord," Serena answered, glancing quickly at Javon and giving him a hopeful grin.

"We removed the bullet in her chest. I'll tell you, she's fortunate it just missed her lungs. But there was no serious damage, and she's good, still recovering, but resting comfortably."

"Amen," answered the woman, now beginning to fidget in her chair, more from excitement than anything else, the doctor thought.

"The bullet that entered her head is another story," said Dr. Rick. "It missed her brain, and we feel it's safely lodged in an area where it won't do any damage. In cases like this, we've had good success just leaving it there. The danger from removing it is far greater than the bullet itself. So, we want to leave it alone. I think it will be safe for years to come...probably for the rest of her life.

"We feel Melissa will make a full recovery."

Serena's eyes darkened. "*But...*" she asked.

"But?"

"Come on, Doctor, there has to be a 'but.' People don't say things the way you just said them unless you were leading up to some big fat 'BUT.'

"So, tell me, Doctor. What is it?"

Dr. Rick moved closer to the woman and sat beside her. He looked at his hands for a moment, then smiled back at her. Serena thought it was a sincere smile, one that she trusted despite his demeanor, which was far too "educated" for her tastes.

"We noticed something else," he said.

Serena immediately panicked. "Like...like cancer?"

"No, Mrs. Washington." the doctor answered. "Something good, something positive, but very rare. It's just that your daughter has a really unusual condition... but in a good way. We want to send her to a specialist in these kinds of cases... so that she can look at it."

Serena seemed relieved, then concerned, then suddenly unreadable. And it was at this moment that

Nurse Tracy entered the room. She glanced at Rick and immediately read the situation.

"It's like this, Mrs. Washington," she said. "Think of it as though Melissa has a very unusual brain, one that's special, with all kinds of great possibilities, one that could help us all but needs to be studied."

The woman smiled, but it was now a mistrustful smile. "You're saying she's a genius?"

"Not exactly," said Rick.

"Not exactly a genius," said Melissa's mother. "But someone special... whose brain they need to study."

Dr. Rick nodded.

"And where are these experts? The University of Rochester? John-Hopkins? Harvard?"

"The only real expert in this field is at Leland University," said Dr. Rick.

"Leland University...and where exactly is that?"

"Palo Alto, California," he answered.

"All the way across the country?"

"Near San Francisco."

"So, you want to take my little girl away from me so they can study her brain at a hospital all the way across the country?"

"We won't take her away from you at all," said Dr. Rick.

"Doctor, did you see the movie Firestarter?" Serena asked.

Tracy spoke up. "I read the book...by Stephen King, right?"

"Yes," the young mother said. ""A government study where they imprison a little girl, isolate her from her family, and do weird experiments on her for a very long time."

"We won't isolate Melissa," said Dr. Rick. "In fact, we've spoken to the doctor in question, and she's already offered to fly you and your son to San Francisco so you can be with Melissa while they see to her. There *will* be testing, but nothing that could endanger her physically."

40

"And you'll have full right of refusal in anything they plan to do."

"It will be a fairly short stay," added Terry. "No more than a month."

Serena's eyes lit up. "A month in San Francisco," she said as she eyed her son.

"All expenses paid," added Dr. Rick. "A nice on-campus residence to stay in."

Mother and son smiled at each other.

"Baby, I always wanted to visit San Francisco, didn't you?"

Javon nodded enthusiastically.

"So, now," Serena asked as she turned back to the doctor with a much more businesslike expression. "When can I see my little girl?"

FOUR—WENTWORTH & KELLY
(Leland, California)

1

Dr. Samuel Wentworth was a seventy-year-old PH.D. Research Department Head at Leland University. As the principal investigator of the Institute for Paleoanthropology Study, he interfaced with the university provost, controlled the budget, managed a small staff of researchers, and directed all projects and activities.

What very few members of the faculty and none of the students knew was that he also wrote romance novels. In fact, behind his desk, a long shelf displayed his self-published works, with covers showing handsome couples clinging desperately to each other as they looked out across windswept landscapes.

Yes, Sam had written over one hundred novellas, and all were embarrassingly erotic. In fact, at that very moment, he was typing away furiously, entering the text of his latest steamy romance, which began:

PARKER'S TRAGIC ROMANCE

Parker Ashley stood in the middle of Times Square, staring at her cell phone.

And then she began shaking it.

"Damn. It's dead... stone cold dead," she murmured." So now I'll never be able to find my way back to my apartment."

New in town, unfamiliar with the streets of New York, uncomfortable in the too-tight white cotton blouse and pencil skirt her friend Sarah had recommended for her first day at the

office, Parker whispered
to her phone,

"Come on, baby. Come
back to life. I need you."

And then an unfamiliar
male voice spoke up from
behind her, "Can I help
you, Miss?"

Parker turned and
looked up into the soft
blue eyes of a tall,
handsome stranger with a
rugged jaw and earnest
smile...

And her heart melted.

Dr. Kathleen Kelly—better known to everyone she
worked with as Dr. K—approached the heavy glass door
to her boss's office. A smile reached her eyes as she
tapped lightly.

Sam looked up.

K was nearly forty, but still as enthusiastic as the day
he had met her and taken her under his wing, a

beautiful young intern with a sweet smile, auburn hair, and endless enthusiasm.

It was all so long ago. And so much had passed between them in the intervening years: Samuel championing her most ambitious projects and getting them funded, his sudden promotion to head of the institute, and K's frenzied efforts to stay with him when some crazy reorg threatened to move her into a separate organization. It was all just academic politics, and Sam was a master. So, they had survived.

"Come on in," he growled happily. "Door's open."

K ducked inside, holding up her iPhone, pointing to the screen, and almost jumping up and down in enthusiasm.

"Our first one," she said. "This girl can come to Leland. Stay for a month, Sam! THIRTY DAYS! What could be better?"

At this point, the old man was frantically trying to save his latest chapter, so he could give K his full attention. Finally, she looked away from her phone long enough to notice what he was doing.

"Writing another dirty book?" she asked as she put her hand on her hip and stared at the old man with gentle accusation.

Samuel blushed, and K couldn't help but wonder how someone so intelligent could write that kind of stuff.

"Are you a romanticist or a smut peddler?" she teased.

Sam looked back defiantly and simply said, "I'm an artist. Now... what ya got?"

"Take a look," K said, turning her phone to the older man. It was an image of a pretty teenage girl with black skin, natural hair, and a sweet but confident look in her eyes.

"She was wounded in a random shooting a few days ago," K said. "Taken to Strong Memorial Hospital in Rochester, New York. She's okay, recovering nicely, but the bullet's still in her head."

Sam just shook his head and sighed as K continued without even taking a breath.

"They did the MRI, and the local staff decided it would be safer to leave the bullet where it was. But then they found this!"

K swiped her thumb across the iPhone screen, flipping to the next image and showing her boss an MRI of the girl's brain. It had very unusual physiology.

Samuel moved to the front of his desk, took the phone, and looked more closely at the image.

"And she can come here?"

"For a month."

"What about her parents; can we get the necessary approvals?"

"Single mom," K answered as she took the phone and pushed it into her pocket. "She wants to come too. So does the girl's younger brother. I'd like to put them all up on campus."

"Are they from the inner city?" asked Samuel.

"Apparently, the worst part of town."

The old man gave his protégé a sarcastic grin. "So, they might actually *enjoy* Leland campus housing."

K raised her eyebrows as she shared the expression. "It's possible."

"Okay," Sam said with a fatherly smile. "Sounds like it's definitely worth doing. Put together a formal request, and I'll make it happen."

2

THREE WEEKS LATER

Dr. K pushed open the door to the campus apartment, and Melissa peered inside.

"Mmmmm," was all she said, even though K could see the eagerness in her eyes.

"She doesn't feel quite ready to enter," the doctor thought. But then Melissa's mom charged past K and right into the room, swinging two big, blue, hard-sided suitcases enthusiastically.

"This will do...this will *definitely* do," said Serena. "Don't you think so, Missy?"

48

"I like it," the girl answered as she moved into the living room, taking in the comfortable-looking couch, the large television, and the ornate lamps on the end tables.

"Nice," she said.

Javon came next, backing into the room, carrying the front end of a large trunk. Their university limo driver, Mr. Henry Fellows (a twenty-five-year Leland employee), held the opposite end.

"Into the bedroom, if you please," said Serena as she pointed into the hallway.

"Uh, which one?" asked Fellows.

"There's more than one?" asked Javon, almost dropping his end of the trunk in surprise.

"There are three," said Dr. K, "One for each of you."

"Trunk goes into *my* room, of course," said Serena.

"The *primary* bedroom then," said K.

Javon was back moments later. "My room is so *dope,*" he said. "Looks down onto three basketball courts. Dudes down there shootin' hoops right now. Could be fun."

"If they let you play," cautioned Serena. "These are college kids, baby...why would they want a sixth-grader in the mix?"

"Just because they're nice," said Melissa with a bright-eyed smile.

"Well, we don't want to assume anything," said Serena. "I've heard college kids can be a little uppity."

"I'm sure they'd be happy to have you participate, Javon," said Dr. K.

"And, besides, I know several of the boys," added Henry as he returned from the bedroom. "I can introduce you to them, and maybe both of us can get into the game. They might appreciate some fresh talent. How's your three-point shot, kid?"

"Awesome," said Javon.

"Thought so," said Henry.

"So, let's check out *your* room, Melissa," said K as she took the girl by the hand and led her into the second bedroom.

"So cool," sighed Missy even before K turned on the lamp, and a silver glow suddenly flashed in the girl's eyes, even more visible now when the lights came on. Hadn't anyone noticed it before? K wondered.

Missy sat on the queen-sized bed that filled the center of the room.

"So soft," she sighed as she bounced up and down. "Never had a bed like this before. I like it."

"And so much closet space," she added, taking in the half-open sliding glass doors that showed enough room to accommodate the wardrobes of *several* Leland freshmen.

"I could stay here forever," she sighed. "Thank you, Doctor."

K moved slowly to the girl and took her hand. "Believe me, Melissa, you'll earn your stay. There's a lot of work for us to do together."

Missy turned serious for a moment. "What kind of work? Will it hurt?"

"Of course not." Answered K." In fact, it should be fun."

"Okay then," the girl answered. "Though I could even put up with a little *hurt*... for all this."

3

"So, let's start with a few questions, okay?" K asked Melissa.

They sat in one of the small conference rooms in the Leland Medical Center. A window beside them offered a view of the brilliant day outside.

K set her iPhone to "record" and placed it in the center of the table.

"This okay with you?" she asked.

The girl nodded. She was smiling, one knee tucked under her, her elbow on the table, her head resting on her hand. She wore a bulky, cardinal-red Leland sweatshirt, which K had just bought for her when she took the Washington family on a campus tour. A cup of hot chocolate sat steaming in front of the girl.

K smiled. "Okay, here goes."

Melissa gave her a slight smile and nodded.

"Let's start with something simple. How do you like the campus?"

Melissa's smile grew. "Awesome."

"What do you like best?"

"So far...just how green everything is. The place is so peaceful. Even with everyone rushing around, it still seems like—you know—*calm*."

"Interesting," said K. "And did you like your home in Rochester?"

The girl shook her head quickly. "Not so much. The kids were rough, and it wasn't safe."

"So then, were you *afraid?*"

Melissa hadn't moved, just sat there, head resting against her hand, those silvery, bright eyes peering back at the doctor.

"No, not afraid, not really."

"You were in danger. But you weren't afraid?"

Melissa finally twisted in her chair, put both feet flat on the floor, and squared her shoulders. "I knew we could handle it."

"We?"

"*Me*. I could handle it."

"Could your mom?"

"She's really tough," the girl said. "But no, she couldn't. Still, I knew I could take care of her."

Melissa's eyes drifted to the window, looking down at the small quadrangle outside. It was sunny out there. The grass smelled sweet and freshly mown, and giant eucalyptus trees towered protectively over everything. Still, when Melissa looked back at K, her expression was troubled.

"I *think* I can take care of my mom," she said. "I hope so."

"You're not sure?"

Melissa reached for the cup of chocolate. She pulled it to her but didn't lift it to her lips.

"No. Not sure, not sure about taking care of Javon either."

"So, you *are* afraid then?"

The girl shrugged nervously.

"Not afraid for myself. But for my family. And not really afraid... more like *uncertain.*"

"I understand," said K as she studied the girl, who returned her gaze evenly.

"Okay. Let's see here," she said as she pulled her iPad to her, continuing to record but also pulling up the list of questions she'd prepared. Then, turning back to the girl, she asked, "Did some of the bigger kids ever try to bully you?"

Melissa smiled. "They tried."

"How?"

"They just got all around me one day when I was walking home. Some of them kept bumping into me, trying to knock me over. Then a couple of bigger kids tried to grab my backpack. I don't know what they thought was in it, but—you know—I held onto it."

"Go on," said K.

"Then, one big kid came up, stood toe to toe with me, and just, like, GROWLED."

Melissa started to giggle. "Like—you know—GROWWWWWWLLLLLL!!!"

K giggled too. She couldn't help it. "And then what?"

"I laughed at him, is all," said Melissa. "But then he pulled back his fist like he was going to punch me. And I gave him my *look*...you know my look." And the girl set her jaw and narrowed her eyes, and that silver glow flashed from them menacingly.

K shifted in her chair. The image Missy described frightened her. "Did he punch you, sweetheart?"

"No," answered Melissa. "The look scared him. I could feel my body turning really solid...hard."

"Rigid?"

"That's it, and I knew my eyes were flaming at him with anger, saying don't you touch me, boy. Don't you DARE touch me."

"And then?"

"He turned and ran away."

"Of course, it happened again when I was walking home with Javon."

"Someone growled at you?"

Melissa laughed out loud. "No way. No. He threatened us, said he was going to tear us apart...or something worse than that. But I just stood there, took Javon's hand, held it, and stood there. And then I could feel the anger glowing in my eyes. It's like I was becoming a stone statue that could resist anything. And my eyes were screaming at him, like, Dude... **LEAVE US ALONE.**"

That glow was back in Melissa's eyes, and it even frightened K as she sat across from the girl.

"And did he leave you alone?"

Melissa smiled again. "Yeah, he did."

"What a relief," K sighed as she noticed the beads of sweat that had formed on her forehead.

She looked at her iPad again and found the next question.

"How did you get shot?"

"What do you mean?"

"You know. Can you describe what happened?"

"Not really," the girl answered. "It was a drive-by."

K swiped the screen of her iPad several times and came up with a front-page newspaper article from the Rochester Democrat and Chronicle. The headline read, "TEENS WOUNDED IN DRIVE BY SHOOTING." She showed the headline to Melissa.

"Did you see this article?"

The girl shook her head.

"It says you and some friends, including your brother, were out in the street one evening. Some of the older neighborhood kids were talking on the stoop behind you. It was getting dark when a beat-up old black car drove up and stopped. Someone leaned out the window and fired six shots, hitting two teenage boys, another girl, and you. You were the most seriously wounded."

Melissa had turned away again and was looking out of the window.

"Missy?" Dr. K said, and the girl turned back to her. "Did you ever think that maybe they were trying to kill YOU?"

She didn't answer.

"I mean, they stopped right in front of *you*, fired at you *first* and then at the teens up on the stoop.

The girl shrugged. "I guess. I mean, I don't know. But maybe...maybe they were."

"Why would they do that?" asked K.

Melissa shrugged.

"Don't know...maybe just because they knew I wasn't afraid of them... and that look of mine... they thought it was dangerous."

4

When Melissa and Dr. K returned to the campus apartment where the Washington family stayed, they found Serena sitting by the window, staring out at the campus. As they entered, she turned to them.

"How'd it go?" she asked in a voice far softer than usual. K noticed the tone but didn't comment; just said, "Very well, thanks. Your daughter is teaching us so much."

"Really," asked Serena with perhaps a hint of irony. "Teaching you about what?"

K approached the woman and sat on the couch across from her.

"She tells me how she's growing up, what she likes, what she doesn't... things like that."

Serena responded with a no-nonsense look. "Well, yeah, of course, *that*," she said. "But Melissa IS different from the rest of us, isn't she?"

K tilted her head slightly and gave Serena a questioning look. "Not completely, no."

"Come on, Doc. My little girl IS DIFFERENT...VERY DIFFERENT," Serena answered anger suddenly flashing in her eyes.

"You know it, I know it; everyone in our damn neighborhood knew it. And I'm afraid some of them wanted to kill her because of IT."

K faced the younger woman. "I don't think…." she began.

"I don't care what you think," Serena interrupted. "You know she is…uh…" – Serena suddenly stopped, searching for the right word – "GIFTED. You know Missy is gifted. And yet you're going to risk her life by sending her back to that hell hole."

"It's your home," K said, knowing that the idea sounded lame.

"But can't we stay here when all this studying is over?"

"I'm sorry," said Dr. K. "But we'll want to *continue* studying Missy in her natural environment."

Tears flashed into Serena's eyes, accompanied by almost unbearable anger.

"She's not some bug for you to study, Doctor. And you know the inner city ain't no damn terrarium.

There's nothing natural about *that* environment. It just puts us all in danger."

"I know," answered K as she sunk back into the coach, lowered her gaze, and didn't see or hear Melissa enter the room.

"MOMMA," the girl said. "STOP IT. I don't want you predicting the future...pretending you know what's going to happen to us. You always do that."

"Do what?"

"Predict, Mom, like you're looking into a crystal ball or something,"

Melissa came up to her mother and took her hand. "You pretend you know exactly what's going to happen. You worry about it so much that it's all you ever think about. And it's...it's always the worst possible thing you can imagine.

"It doesn't have to be that way, Mom. Everything can turn out okay, honest."

Serena squeezed her daughter's hand and stared at her with tears in her eyes.

"Not if we have to go back to the neighborhood, baby. Not if we end up back where those hoods are trying to murder you. Don't you understand, girl? They want to kill you."

Serena turned back to Dr. K with a look that begged the woman to find a safer place for them to live. And K did want to help this desperate young family. But she knew that removing the girl from her environment would be to intervene and possibly change what was happening to her. Still, she was about to answer Melissa's mom when the door to the room suddenly burst open, and Javon breezed in carrying a basketball. Henry was right behind him.

"What a game!" he called.

"Those college kids got nothin' on you, boy," added Henry as he turned and gave Javon a spirited high-five.

"I love it here!" said the boy. "I never want to leave. This is the place for me...and for all of us."

5

PARKER'S TRAGIC ROMANCE

Parker stood outside her midtown office building in a heavy downpour, jostled on all sides by co-workers who were bigger and more aggressive than she was. Finally, still fighting with her soggy umbrella, she dared to step right out into the middle of the busy street and hail a cab. The driver saw her and raced past six men and a trio of women to stop right in front of her.

Parker smiled gratefully and reached for the door handle. But then a masculine hand grabbed it before she could, and Parker looked up to see a handsome young man jerk open the door and usher his pregnant and very wet wife inside.

"Rat-fuck!" mumbled Parker, wondering what corner of her childhood playground experience brought that phrase to mind.

But now another taxi raced directly in front of her and stopped. She reached for the door handle again, only to see another male hand beat her to it.

"Rat..." Parker began when a more forceful hand grabbed the interloper by the wrist and jerked him away.

Parker looked up to see a man standing there, smiling at her...the same handsome guy who had helped her find her way home on her first day in New York.

He opened the door for Parker and, in the process, blocked anyone who might have tried to steal her ride.

Once inside, Parker rolled down the window and gave him her very best smile. "You saved me again," she said.

"Guess it's my job," he said, reaching inside and offering his hand...it was much more than a handshake. Parker thought. And then, just as the taxi pulled away, the handsome stranger looked after her and shouted, "Name's Jason Preston...don't forget."

How could she? Parker thought. HOW COULD SHE?

"So..." Samuel said anxiously... "How do you like it?"

K held the newest pages of her friend's romance novel away from her, knowing that her answer meant a great deal to him. Damn...did she really want to tell the truth?

"Well, you know, Sam, I'm just not the right audience for this. You're already on the best-seller list. So, why ask me?"

Samuel lowered his eyes in disappointment. "Just wanted your educated opinion," he said. "Most women love this stuff."

"Right. But—you know—I'm not most women."

"You never have romantic fantasies?" he asked with a twinkle returning to his eyes.

K laughed, "Not lately. I've too much on my mind."

Samuel rolled his chair back and stood up slowly. "Yeah, about that," he said. "Is there any way I can help?"

"It's just...Melissa and her family," K said. "We pulled them out of the most dangerous part of the inner city, and now we have to send them back."

Samuel took the pages from K and tossed them back onto his desk. Then he took a seat near her and crossed his arms.

"Why send them back?"

K ran the fingers of both hands through her auburn hair. She shook it free for a moment and sighed. "Can't mess with evolution, can we, Sam?"

"Why not?" he said. "If these kids are an evolutionary leap, the way we think they are, it would be impossible for us to affect it." He laughed and shook his head. "That idea is even more ridiculous than my romances."

K tried to smile. "Not sure about that."

The old man stood then, approached K, took her hand, and knelt beside her. Now his words were gentle.

"If we know anything, K, it's that you can't screw up evolution. It's something that operates independently, by its own rules, in its own time… and that's thousands of years. So, nothing we do will affect it."

K looked into Samuel's eyes. He nodded, and so did she. "Maybe you're right."

"Of course, I am."

"So, you're saying I should let the family stay here, maybe find them a permanent place to live?"

"Why not? Help them out. Look at this." And he held up two MRIs, one of Melissa's brain and one from another patient.

"Melissa here," he said, raising one image higher. "That little girl who came to the ER after her skiing accident, Sandra Brown, here." See the difference?"

"A much smaller lizard brain in Missy," said K. "Much lower instinct for fight or flight...much less panic, much less fear, much less negative response."

"No single act can change the results of thousands of years of evolution. Likewise, a single change in environment won't make any difference at this point. So do whatever you want. It may complicate your study a little, but that's okay. Give the girl's family a home right here. I'll talk to the provost about it. We can find the bucks to cover the costs for a little while, anyway.

"And, while we're doing that, keep watching. I'll be interested to see what you find out. There are plenty of other examples of this new species anyway."

"Yes, I know," said K. "Several more have come to my attention, and I plan to start tracking them."

"Good. Let's learn more about these creatures, whatever you call them...."

"I like to call them Evolution's Angels," said K.

Sam grimaced and then became thoughtful.

"You really want to go there. You're inviting in the Christian Right and might complicate your research with side issues that don't really matter."

"The name just came to me one morning after a mostly sleepless night," answered K. "Seemed right at the time... hate to give it up now."

"I know the feeling," said Sam.

"An intuitive flash mixing science and inspiration."

"WOW! Who would want to quelch that. Okay, why not? Let's see what one example of these new angels of yours does when she's transported from a toxic environment to a safe one."

"Thanks," K said, and she stood and helped Samuel to his feet.

"I'll go give Serena the good news."

"Great," he answered. "And, while you're at it, think about whatever new capabilities these kids might reveal."

"What are you talking about?" K asked, not sure the old man was being serious.

"You know, do they have superpowers? Can they fly, mind meld, see through walls?"

"There's no evidence of any of that."

"No, but your sample is tiny. Keep your eyes open. You may have only scratched the surface."

"Sounds like more of your fiction, Doctor," said K.

Samuel shrugged, smiled, and then added, "You never know, do you?"

FIVE—ÁNGEL
(Outside Tucson, Arizona)

1

Firefighter Lucas Antone eyed the picture of his niece taped to the dashboard of his big Ram truck. It was a copy of the portrait his friend Antonio Rivera had made for the local casino. The image was part of an enormous billboard on the highway leading up to the place... a message about the use of casino profits... a large part went for the education of kids on the reservation.

The little girl looked so damn cute, with huge dimples and laughing eyes...who could resist? Who wouldn't mind losing a few bucks to help educate a kid like her?

Lucas wanted the picture with him so he could see it every day, remind him of his family, even on his way up the dirt roads to the fire lookout he had to man three days a week. The actual painting hung on the wall of the firehouse, just across from his bunk. It was a sobering influence on a barracks full of rough men, maybe, but what was wrong with that? So far, no one had asked him to take it down.

Lucas realized he was getting distracted. He didn't want anything to prevent him from doing his job or missing important happenings around him. Of course, there wasn't much to see in this desert country... just dry hills, parched earth, little or no water, swirling dust. But he did spot one of Antonio Rivera's wells as he passed. Ángel and Antonio were standing beside the round wall of stone, peering into it, arguing—as if a boy had a right to argue with his grandfather, Lucas thought. But he was.

And then Lucas saw the old man step into the well, descending quickly down the steps inside.

What was the point, the fireman wondered. Everyone knew there was no water down there. But, hell, there wasn't any water anywhere at this elevation.

A bend in the highway took Lucas in a different direction, about to cut off his view of the well, the boy, and the old man, when he saw Ángel turn to the Jeep they'd come in.

Lucas thought there must be someone in the old four-wheeler because the last thing he could make out was the Jeep starting up and driving quickly up to the well. Must be one of the ranch hands, Lucas said to the pretty picture of little Talley.

But he was wrong.

2

"I want to make sure it's totally dry," Antonio had said to his grandson. "If there's even a trickle down there, we should nurture it... anything for our land and cattle."

"Be careful, Papa," the boy had said in the flat voice he always used when he spoke of something that might scare the hell out of anyone else. "The last time I was down there, the lower steps were already gone."

"Trust me, I know what I'm doing," said the old man as he reached forward and ruffled the boy's hair. Then he threw his leg over the side of the well and began to climb down.

But then, only a few steps in, his heel hit the side of the well where the steps had ended. He toppled away from the wall barely able to grab onto the last rung of the ladder and hang there.

"Mother of God," the old man called. "Here, boy, give me a hand."

Ángel reached quickly for his grandfather... but really, what were the chances of a twelve-year-old holding onto a man who weighed over a hundred pounds? Antonio swung one hand toward Ángel while he tried to maintain his grasp on the steps with the other. Unfortunately, they missed the connection, and Antonio was able to hang on for about ten more seconds before he plummeted into the empty well.

Antonio slammed his shoulder into the brutally hard well bottom, cried out in pain, and lay there, knowing his whole right side had been crushed.

Ángel heard the cry and turned at once to the Jeep, narrowing his silvery eyes and insisting that it come to life and drive directly to him.

It did.

Next, with that same willpower, the boy forced the back of the Jeep to open and directed a long rope out of the vehicle and into the well, where the end of the rope sought out the old man who lay on the floor.

"Let it tie around you, Papa," the boy called as he directed the rope to fasten itself under the old man's arms while he ran to the Jeep and made sure that the rope was secured to the back bumper.

Then, again looking into the well, Ángel directed the Jeep—without actually driving it—to slowly reverse and raise the injured old man up the side of the well.

The boy caught his grandfather at the very top and helped him pull one leg and then the other over the rim.

"By Jesus," said Antonio, as he lay panting beside the well, "how did you ever do all that? Did you drive the Jeep yourself?"

"I had to," said Ángel matter-of-factly. "So, I did."

3

The boy and his grandfather heard the roar of the pickup truck as it climbed to the well, and Lucas got out.

"I saw you boys as I drove by a while ago," he said. "I was afraid something might go wrong when you climbed into the well, Antonio. That's why I doubled back."

"I fell in," grumbled the old man. "But Ángel here is a special kid, you know that don't you? He brought the jeep to the well and pulled me out."

Ángel shrugged. "Had to save Papa."

Lucas pulled his big cowboy hat from his head and swiped his brow. "How the hell..." he began. Then added, "Well, his name *is* Ángel, so I guess he could work a miracle or two if he had to."

4

"A mind-meld with a machine," Lucas told the doctor. "Still can't believe it."

They brought Antonio to the same hospital that treated Ángel when he fell from his horse. Dr. Cynthia Scott was an original member of the team that saw his MRI, noted the unusual physiology of his brain, and eventually reported it to Dr. K at Leland. But she still felt skeptical about Lucas's latest observations.

"The unusual configuration of Ángel's brain is obvious to anyone who looks at his MRI," she said. "We all saw it, repeated the procedure, and saw it again. then we learned about Dr. K's research at Leland and decided to let her know about Ángel.

"I guess she's coming out here to interview him in a few days."

Lucas didn't know about any of that; he wasn't much into *'unusual physiology,'* as Dr. Scott called it. "But still," he said, "Ángel has the ability to move things with his mind? How?"

"What you describe doesn't sound like telekinesis," answered the doctor, "where individuals just *move* objects with the power of their minds. You're suggesting that the boy actually operated a piece of equipment remotely without being at the controls.

"Even comic book superheroes aren't supposed to be able to do that."

"Mind-meld with a machine," repeated Lucas, "like the two of them are brothers...like me and my truck."

"Except you can't start your truck with your mind," said Dr. Scott, "and you certainly can't drive it across town without being in it, then pick up your fiancée, and bring her back to you—again only controlling your truck with the power of your mind. It's like Ángel's brain just eliminated the need for the key, the gas pedal, the steering wheel, and the brake."

"And the driver," Lucas added.

The boy watched and listened as the two adults talked about him. But he really didn't care what they were saying. He was tired and worried about his grandfather. And, as far as his ability to control machines with his mind? Hey, he needed to do it, and so he did.

Ángel knew the Jeep was standing by. Somehow, the vehicle had made it clear to him, almost advising him that it was ready. So Ángel just took over. No big deal.

5

"You gotta see this kid," Dr. Scott said to K.

They were speaking FaceTime through their cell phones: Cynthia in her office cubicle at the Tucson Hospital, K on a park bench on the Leland campus.

Cynthia had just relayed Lucas's story about the Jeep and the well and Ángel's apparently magical powers.

"I mean, the only place anyone has ever seen anything like this," said Scott, "is in the movies."

"Like the sorcerer's apprentice moving magical brooms to wash the floor in Fantasia?" asked K. She would have laughed, but it was just a little too unbelievable.

"Not just *moving* the brooms," said Cynthia. "Directing them, putting them to work."

"And was there a gleam in Ángel's eyes when he did it?" asked K. "Kind of a silvery glow that moved inside his iris?"

"I wasn't there...don't know," said Cynthia. "I mean, the boy's eyes have a silver coloring if that's what you mean."

K paused momentarily, watching a small group of students walk by carrying computer tablets under their arms. One even had a big old hardcover book that weighed more than all the computers combined. Times were evolving...and so, apparently, was the human species. But this was so much more than the gradual slog of evolution. This was a gigantic evolutionary jump forward that seemed to have happened almost instantly.

"Okay, I'll be coming to Tucson as soon as I can.," said K. "I'll want to talk to Lucas, Ángel, and maybe the grandfather too, if he's okay."

"Tough old dude," said Dr. Scott. "He took quite a fall and fractured his shoulder, but he's still awake, responsive, and even optimistic."

"Sounds good," said K. "If you don't mind. I'd like to bring Samuel along."

"Speaking of tough old dudes," said Dr. Scott. "It will be good to see him in the flesh. I hear he writes romance novels."

"Are you a reader?" asked K.

"I can be."

"Well, I'd steer clear of Sam's work. I mean, I love him dearly, but his romances are just over the top."

"In what way?"

"ALL ways," answered K. "Just be forewarned. In any case, I'll text you as soon as I can arrange a flight."

"Yes, thanks."

K. ended the conversation, and an hour later, she sat at the kitchen table in Melissa's campus apartment...performing part of what had become daily observation.

In another room, the girl, her mother, and her brother watched TV, flipping through channels and checking out various sports shows.

K's eyes drifted down to the tabletop ...to the remote control sitting there. She picked it up, realizing that university housing didn't provide more than one remote control per television.

Serena certainly wouldn't have spent money to buy another remote, would she? Definitely not. Someone just left the remote in the kitchen. So, how were they controlling the television in the other room?

K took the remote, got to her feet, and moved slowly up behind the family. Then, she pointed the remote at the television, and suddenly turned the set off.

"What the???" called Javon in alarm. "Hey...I was really getting into that show."

K didn't say anything, hoping no one noticed her. But Melissa just shrugged, and the TV came back on.

"That's not the right channel," said Javon.

"Sorry," said the girl, "the stupid television does that sometimes." And, without even moving, Melissa switched to the show they had been watching.

"Damn," murmured K. "She can do it too."

She knew she had no real evidence that Melissa or the other "special" kids could control machines with their minds...until now.

K had the report about the boy in Arizona. And now, several hundred miles away, a girl from Upstate New York changed channels without a remote.

Did that prove anything?

"Well," K whispered to herself, "a television is really a machine, isn't it? In many ways, it isn't that different from a truck."

SIX—KATHLEEN
(Leland, California)

1

PARKER'S TRAGIC ROMANCE

The doors of the small midtown Manhattan bar blew open, and two extremely handsome young men entered. One was tall, dark, and Italian-looking, with a face that was almost too pretty. The other, an African American, was broad-shouldered and could have been a professional linebacker...but with the intelligent smile of a science teacher. At least, that's what Parker thought.

The men clearly hit the gym every day of the week.

Perfect physiques filled their tight t-shirts, sports coats, and slacks. For a moment, Parker was glad Bridget had talked her into wearing the infamous little black dress she'd bought for her first night on the town. The neckline was so low that Parker didn't dare lean forward. And the dress was so short that she kept shifting back and forth in her seat, tugging on the hem, trying to be as modest as possible.

"Don't do that," whispered Bridget across the cocktails in front of them. "You're just drawing attention to yourself. And your legs are gorgeous. Every guy here would love to have them wrapped around him."

"BRIDGET!" Parker responded in shock.

"What? Relax, girl. This is supposed to be fun.

Remember? and look. Those two gorgeous guys who just walked in are staring at us."

Parker glanced over at the men who were smiling at them eagerly. And then she jumped back, almost spilling her drink in the process.

"Oh, my God!" Parker gasped. "It's HIM! IT'S JASON!!"

Samuel's smile was just too self-satisfied, K thought, as he sat behind his computer finishing the latest chapter in his romance novel. But hey, maybe he felt so successful that this was a good time to ask him about visiting Tucson. He could help interview the boy who apparently drove cars with his mind.

In any case, she thought it was definitely best not to mock Samuel's hobby right now... best not to mention it at all if possible. But then she did.

"Like what you've written?" she asked, standing well away from the computer so she wouldn't embarrass the old man by reading over his shoulder.

Samuel's eyes brightened. "Really great," he said. "Can I print you out a copy?"

K panicked.

"GOD, NO!" she almost blurted but caught herself just in time.

"Maybe on the plane," she said with a forced smile.

The old man's eyes darkened. "Going somewhere?"

"Yeah, Tucson. There's a twelve-year-old boy there, already in our database. He's exhibiting some unusual characteristics...maybe new manifestations of a new species. I've picked up traces of them in Melissa as well. Glad you talked me into keeping her here with us."

Samuel slid his chair over so K could sit beside him. His latest manuscript was closed, the computer showing nothing but an image of Leland's Main Quad.

"What kind of characteristics are you talking about?" he asked. "What would you call them?"

K closed her eyes, thought for a moment, bit her lip, and then just said what she thought was the most accurate description. "I'd say they were magical."

"What?"

"You know, like in the movie *Fantasia*?"

"You mean ordering a brigade of mops and buckets to wash the floor?" Sam said.

"Exactly...sort of," said K. "The kids are starting to act like human remote controls, turning things on and off with their minds."

2

San Francisco International Airport was as crowded as K and Samuel had ever seen it. Even passengers with preferred seating faced long lines before they could clear TSA and enter the boarding area.

Both doctors had small carry-on bags for the four-day stay they planned in Tucson. After all, Ángel hadn't been hurt in the incident at the well. He just displayed

some unusual—no, let's call them what they were—
unbelievable abilities.

Politely, Samuel stepped back like a gentleman from
one of his romance novels and let his female companion
go first. Never mind that K had surpassed his academic
ranking and position in the medical research staff.
Samuel insisted on observing the protocols of chivalry
whether K wanted him to or not.

Of course, it was Samuel's carry-on that was sent
through the scanner three times for some unidentified
liquid detected deep in a hidden pocket. It turned out to
be the old man's personal mix of mouthwash, created
by blending four different brands to come up with his
ideal flavor for morning gargling.

K rolled her eyes. *Men*, she thought...the superior
sex...yeah right.

When she imagined getting married, which she did
less and less, it was certainly not to a man like this:
funky and fastidious, not to mention well over seventy.
Twenty years earlier—there had been some speculation

on the part of their colleagues that there could be a budding romance between them. Samuel might have thought it possible too. But then K showed up at a faculty get-together with Theodocia Witherspoon, an old college roommate K had had a brief fling with senior year. Thea, as K called her, allowed the new doctor to show the entire medical staff that her preferences were not entirely heterosexual.

But then, two weeks later, K unceremoniously rejected the first *female* colleague from Leland to suggest that she and K have a liaison. K was monogamous, she said...or at least *"taken by Thea,"* whenever her college friend came to town.

What K really wanted was simply to be left alone...no romance and no drama. And only one person ever figured it all out...Sam.

"So, I've been thinking about these angels of yours," he said as he and K took their seats in the boarding area.

"And????" K asked. Romance novelist or not, she respected Samuel as a scientist and a researcher.

Samuel leaned back in the uncomfortable airport seat. "I think the one thing that distinguishes *our* current species from all others is our tools."

"Okaaaay..." K answered with a slow nod. "And...."

"Maybe a monkey, a crow, or even a dolphin can grab something and use it as a tool, but we make tools from scratch, design them, *refine* them, and transfer them from one need to another. We turn them into systems, use them for working the fields, building cities, killing anything we decide we need to kill, including each other."

"The romance of tool-making?" K added with a smirk.

"Careful there, Doctor," Sam said jokingly, "or you'll take our whole conversation off course."

"I know," she said as she tried her best for a relatively serious look.

"Think of this," said Samuel. "Maybe our machines are really evolving right along with us."

"Okay."

"Machines and humans...evolving in parallel, even symbiotically."

"Makes sense."

"Little by little, we're discarding the trappings of our animal ancestors, and our minds are taking over. And little by little, machines are discarding their reliance on the creatures that use them."

Sam got that professorial gleam in his eye again. "So then, you tell me, Dr. K. What's next?"

The woman crossed her arms—maybe even crossed her eyes—in frustration. "Tools that run themselves?"

"Convergence, baby," he said. "Man and machine merging...becoming one."

"Super-human robots?"

"Probably something much more elegant than that. But whoever they are, whatever they are, they'll leave us homo sapiens in the dust."

"Jesus, Sam!" said K.

"Yeah, possibly him too."

Samuel closed his eyes, seemed to be thinking deeply, then opened them and smiled at his protégé. "Just a theory, you understand."

3

Dr. Cynthia Scott pulled her grey 2010 Volvo around the circular driveway and up to the old Rivera farmhouse outside Tucson. She stopped the car, and then she and Doctors Kelly and Wentworth emerged from the car's air-conditioned interior and into the blazing Arizona sunshine.

Talley was there in an instant, ready to greet the trio and usher them into the air-conditioned space of the hacienda.

"We've been waiting for you," said the girl as though she were an experienced hostess. "Antonio and

Ángel are in the living room. Mama and I are in the kitchen preparing lunch for everyone."

"Thank you so much," said Dr. Scott.

"Lucas is with Mr. Antonio and Ángel."

"I met your uncle, didn't I?" asked Scott.

"You did. He helped get Mr. Rivera to the hospital after Ángel pulled him from the well...with the Jeep...I guess."

"Of course," said Scott. "Thank you."

They walked quickly to the house, entered through automatic doors, and welcomed the blessedly cool interior. The walls and ceilings of the large entryway were covered with lively and colorful murals depicting life on the ranch.

"Impressive," said K.

"The work of Mr. Rivera, who is a fine artist and a graduate of Chouinard Institute," said Talley.

"And here we are," she concluded as she led the guests into the living room, where Antonio, Lucas, and

Ángel stood as they approached. Next to Ángel stood another boy.

"That's Johnny Norris," added Talley with a touch of disdain in her voice. "He's another kid from the rez...like me."

"But much better looking than you are," Johnny teased.

"Calm down, kids," said Lucas. "Thank you, Talley."

The girl stuck her tongue out at Johnny, then nodded to Lucas, curtsied, and left the room.

Everyone exchanged pleasantries for a brief moment before Sam said, "As exciting as your ranch is, Señor Rivera, we find the recent accomplishments of your grandson even more remarkable."

The old man smiled. "He is quite a boy."

"So, is it all right if we ask him some detailed questions about what happened when you fell into the well?"

Antonio smiled and glanced at Ángel. "Of course."

"But I'm not sure I know what happened," Ángel added.

"I understand," K said with a sympathetic smile. "Still, why don't you try to describe it in your own words, Ángel? Maybe we'll understand things a little better just by the way you tell the story."

The boy shrugged. "Okay."

"But first, please have a seat," said Lucas. "Would any of you like a drink?"

Before anyone could answer, Talley scurried into the room with a tray full of glasses filled with iced tea. She set the tray on the table.

"There's sugar, too," she said, gesturing toward the sugar bowl and spoon in the center of the tray."

"Thank you very much," said Sam. "I like mine unsweetened." And he reached for a glass, took a sip, and smiled. "Hits the spot."

"Thank you, Talley."

The girl nodded, gave Johnny another nasty look, and rushed from the room.

As the others each took a glass of iced tea, with only K and Johnny adding sugar to their drinks, Ángel began.

"We went out to the well because Papa thought it was a...a...*good* well."

"Productive," said Antonio.

"We wanted to find out if there was any water left in there. There was a ladder on the inside with steps leading all the way down to the very bottom. We knew they must be a little worn, but no one had been down to the bottom in years.

"So, Papa decided to climb down."

"Like a fool," said Antonio.

"But the steps gave way," Ángel continued, "and he fell all the way to the bottom. I heard his shoulder crack when it happened."

"And how did you feel at that moment?" K. asked Ángel.

"Like I had to do something."

"You weren't afraid?"

"I wasn't scared...but I knew the Jeep was better for the job than I was."

"Did you think you should drive the Jeep up to the well?"

"The Jeep seemed to want to drive itself. So, I just sort of pictured how to get it done. You know, like using the rope in the back of the Jeep to pull Papa out of the well."

"Then what happened?" asked Samuel.

"The Jeep drove over, the trunk popped open, and the rope snaked out and slid into the well."

"I was in too much pain to object," said Antonio, "but seeing that rope sliding down the side of the wall and coming toward me all by itself...*that* was crazy."

"I told Papa I was using the rope to grab and pull him up to safety."

"Amazing," said Dr. Scott, who, up until this point, had hardly said a word.

"Tell me, Ángel, how did you *control* the rope?" asked K.

Ángel's response was quick and confident. "I didn't control the rope, I just knew that Papa needed to be pulled out of the well, and the rope must have known it too and pretty much did the rest on its own."

Antonio said, "Somehow, it slid under my back and fastened itself under my arms. Then I heard the Jeep revving its engine, and it was pulling me up the side of the well. Very gently, too, I might add."

"Incredible," said Samuel, smiling as he shook his head in wonder.

"Did you think of any other way to try and save your Papa before you called the Jeep?" asked K.

The boy stopped for a moment, staring at the doctor, yet probably not even seeing her. "I did have this idea that I might be able to fly down there, grab him, and carry him back up."

"Really?" asked Samuel. "FLY?"

"I know," answered Ángel as he twisted his face in disbelief. "It didn't make any sense to me either."

"I would have liked to try it," his friend Johnny added. K turned to the boy and noticed suddenly that there was a silvery glow in his eyes as well. She wanted to consider the possibility that he, too, might be one of evolution's angels, but she knew she had to focus on the adventure at the well first. So, she turned to the old man.

"How would you describe *your* experience, Señor Rivera?"

He looked at each doctor, sat forward in his chair, and folded his hands.

"To be honest with you," he said. "It was like being in a cartoon...like when things like teapots and candelabras start dancing, Jeeps and ropes snaking around and saving my life."

K turned to Lucas, who, up to this point, had only listened to the boy and the old man tell of their adventure.

"You saw what happened from some distance away, Lucas," she said. "How would you describe it?"

Lucas leaned toward K and smiled at her. He gave her a silly expression that seemed to ask, "You heard what happened? How could I ever explain something like that?"

Finally, he simply said, "It was magical."

"Magical," repeated K.

"Like a fantasy movie," added Antonio.

"Did any of you," Samuel finally asked, looking from the old man to Lucas, to the boy, "feel that Ángel was *controlling* the rope and the Jeep? Was he telling them what to do with his mind?"

Antonio and Lucas turned and looked at each other.

"He must have been," said Antonio.

SEVEN—LILLIE
(Felicity, California—Northern Sierra Foothills)

1

Four-year-old Lillie Allonzo squatted on the bare sub-floor of the family kitchen. Her parents were busy remodeling the addition after the recent wildfire had severely damaged it.

Adam and his wife Donna had restored the home when they first moved in, turning the neglected old farmhouse into a modern four-bedroom bungalow. They had completely redone the kitchen, bath, and bedrooms, mostly by themselves...learning by doing along the way.

In the wake of the disastrous fire that had nearly destroyed the new kitchen, and—with the help of Donna's brother Jim and a few other friends—they ripped out the damaged kitchen cabinets and tore up the floor. Adam had done a surprisingly good job putting up drywall to replace the cracked and broken plaster, and with everyone's help, they had pulled out all the damaged appliances.

Now, little Lillie had a hammer almost as big as she was, and—using both hands—she was trying to drive a row of nails her dad had started for her into the subflooring. Another layer of flooring would go on top of it.

"The kid can pound away to her heart's content," Adam told his wife. "Any hammer marks she makes will be covered up."

Donna stood in the middle of the room—kerchief wrapped around her forehead to hold back her sweaty hair. Somehow, it still managed to droop down over her eyes. She brushed it back and turned around, looking from one wall to the other. They were all freshly finished by a guy who had never done it before.

"You are one handy carpenter," she giggled as she looked at her husband.

"And you are one sexy apprentice," responded Adam.

"I hope we won't be too tired tonight," Donna giggled. "I want to see just how handy you can be when...."

AND JUST THEN, THE LIGHTS WENT OUT.

"WHEEE, Mommy," Lillie called, sounding both surprised and excited.

"It's okay, baby," said Donna as she picked up her daughter.

"Can't see very well, can we?"

"Daddy will fix it."

But after a moment, Adam said, "Wish I knew how. There's a short in the wiring somewhere, but I can't find it. Neither could the guys who put in the new overhead light. They thought they had...but look." He went to the light switch and flipped it up and down. Nothing happened. "No light here."

106

Lillie began to squirm, and so Donna put her down. She stood beside her mother, holding onto the pocket of her mom's overalls for a moment.

What's she thinking about? Donna wondered as she studied the girl's expression. Lillie had her hand on her chin as though she were a scientist contemplating the order of the universe. Then, the little girl walked slowly toward her father.

It was late evening. Without the overhead lights, the low angle of the sunlight through the windows cast long shadows across the room. In the far corner where Adam stood, there was barely any light at all.

"Daddy?" said Lillie.

"What is it, Honey?"

"Why is it so dark in here?"

Donna giggled. "She has a way with words, doesn't she?"

Adam took the question more seriously. "I'm afraid there's a short somewhere in the wiring," he said. "It could be anywhere."

He wiped his forehead. It was getting damn hot again because the air conditioning had died along with the lights.

"I'm afraid we may have to rip out all the wiring to track down the problem."

"That's not good. Is it, Daddy?"

Adam sighed and squatted in front of his little daughter. "No, honey, it's not. If we can't find the problem in the wires that run across the attic, we may have to rip out the walls, maybe even the flooring to find it."

Lillie put her hand to her chin again—thinking.

"I see," she said. "Okay, I'll help you then."

Donna laughed. "How cute is she?" The young mother could barely make out the silvery flicker in the little girl's eyes as she stood across the room from her.

But then, suddenly...

THE LIGHTS CAME ON.

2

The following morning, Lillie found herself in the attic with her father.

He held a flashlight as he and his daughter crawled along the rough, unfinished studs, following the wires between them.

Why was Lillie with him? Adam wondered. The answer was simple. She wanted to be. And even though she hadn't made a fuss about it, she was very insistent.

Adam inspected a splice where wires were joined, one set splitting off from the main line to feed the outlets and appliances in the room below.

"It all looks good, baby," Adam said as he crawled to the last splice at the far end of the attic. He shined his flashlight onto it. "The connection's perfect," he said.

"Of course it is," said Lillie. "Why wouldn't it be?"

Adam looked at his daughter in surprise. "Because little girls can't fix faulty wiring with their minds?" He said.

Lillie giggled.

"You can't, can you?" Adam asked. "Because I'm afraid that's what your mother is starting to think.

"Don't be silly, Daddy."

Not knowing exactly what that meant, Adam turned and, with Lillie in front of him, began to crawl back over the rough attic studs. They moved slowly toward the opposite wall, where a retractable ladder descended through a framed opening to the hallway below.

"Everything seems fine," Adam told his daughter. "Let's just get out of here."

Lillie crawled ahead of her father until she reached the opposite wall, where a big, open window overlooked their backyard. Adam had opened the window to let in some fresh air because heat was already building in the attic's confined space.

"Hi, Mommy," said the little girl as she waved to Donna, who was watching from outside.

"Lillie, get down here," called Donna. Intending, of course, that her daughter turn around and come down the ladder with her father.

Instead, the little girl suddenly stepped through the open window.

"OH MY GOD!" Donna gasped, sure that Lillie was about to fall to her death.

Instead, she *floated* down from the window, moving gracefully through the air, not exactly flying but traveling in slow motion as though she were controlling her own descent.

"OH, LILLIE," called her mother as she rushed toward the four-year-old, who stepped lightly onto the ground.

"DON'T YOU EVER DO THAT TO ME AGAIN! I could have had a heart attack."

"Okay, Mommy, sorry," said Lillie. "I didn't mean to scare you."

"But you did, baby," Donna answered. "Little girls aren't supposed to be able to float through the air. Who knew you could do that?"

"I did," said Lillie.

Adam was looking down in terror from the window above. He hadn't seen what had happened.

"Is she all right?"

Donna clutched the little girl to her. "Somehow, she's fine. She just floated down from the window as though she was—I don't know—gliding down some invisible escalator."

"Wait there," called Adam, and he turned back to the ladder, descended quickly, and ran out to his wife and daughter. He grabbed Lillie, spun her around, held her at arm's length, and stared into those silvery eyes.

"Honey, you just can't do that."

Lillie smiled questioningly. "Why not?"

"Little girls just can't go around jumping out of windows. You could hurt yourself."

"I really couldn't, daddy," she said. But then, reading the concern on her father's face, she added, "But okay. I'll be more careful."

"Did you *fall* out of the window?" he asked. And Lillie immediately shook her head.

112

"Did you jump?"

Lillie giggled, then shook her head again. "I just... *walked* out of the window."

"She floated down," said Donna. "It was almost magical."

Adam glanced around in total confusion.

"Okay then," he said, brushing his fingers back through his hair in frustration. "No more magic, Lillie. Please."

The little girl smiled sweetly. "Okay, Daddy. I promise."

EIGHT—KATHLEEN
(Felicity, California—Northern Sierra Foothills)

1

Samuel's rickety old Mercedes rolled up in front of *The Sacramento Café* on a bright California morning. He and K got out of the car and turned to see Dr. Paul Grinnell leave his Corvette and walk across the street to greet them.

"K," Dr. Paul said, and she held out her hand. He took it, gave it a squeeze, and then turned to the old man.

"Hey, Bud, been a while."

"Too long," said Samuel. Then, looking around, he added, "And where's our little prodigy?"

""They were just a few minutes behind me," said Dr. Paul. "Let's go inside and get a table. I'm sure they'll be right along."

He led K and Samuel through the café's double doors and into the interior.

The place was sparkly this morning. Sunlight streamed in through the big front window, almost making its way beyond the bar to the very depths of the restaurant. The floor was hardwood. License plates from various western states formed a colorful border along the upper edge of the wall and over the bar, where an aging waitress in a cream-colored dress stood talking to the bartender. The barkeep, also a woman, wore a white Oxford shirt, tie, vest, and black slacks.

"Sit anywhere you like," said the waitress. And, just as Dr. Paul selected a large round table in the back of the room, Adam Alonzo's pick-up pulled into the space beside Samuel's Mercedes.

Moments later, Donna entered the café, leading Lillie by the hand. Adam was right behind them.

"Here, Donna," called Dr. Paul, and she waved and headed in their direction.

"These are Doctors Kathleen Kelly and Samuel Wentworth from Leland University," said Dr. Paul. "And this is the Allonzo Family, Adam, Donna, and Lillie."

Lillie smiled and nodded as the adults shook hands.

"Call me K," said Kathleen as they all found seats around the table.

The waitress was right there with the menus. "Hi, I'm Connie. Can I get you guys anything to drink while you settle in?"

She turned to K first, who ordered an iced tea. "Kind-a parched from the long drive," she added.

"Sounds good, iced tea for me too, and a glass of milk for our little girl," said Donna.

Lillie smiled and nodded. She seemed very happy, as she should be, thought K, knowing the mental and emotional makeup of these angels.

"Black coffee," said Dr. Paul. "Same here," said Adam. "Here too, but with cream and sweetener on the side," added Sam.

"Be right back with your drinks," said Connie, and she disappeared.

"So then, Lillie," K began, smiling warmly at the little girl, "what have you been up to?"

Lillie looked at her mother for a moment, then back at K. "Building our kitchen."

"She's been helping nail down the subflooring," said Adam, and he gave his daughter a proud smile. "And something else," Donna added.

"What's that?" asked Sam.

"You told them about the wiring, right?" she asked Dr. Paul. who nodded.

"It looks like she fixed the electrical wiring in the kitchen all by herself," said the girl's mother, "...with her mind."

"Donna, there are a million explanations for how that wiring could have started working again," said Adam.

"Don't think so."

"And when did you get your contractor's license?" her husband asked.

There was a brief stand-off between the two parents when K suddenly spoke up.

"And what do you say, Lillie?"

All eyes turned to the little girl. She shrugged and began fidgeting with the place setting in front of her.

"Did you do anything to fix the wiring in the kitchen?" K asked.

Lillie turned her fork around, so the prongs faced the table's edge and the handle pointed away from her. She looked up, eyed each of the adults, and then turned the fork back around.

"You don't have to answer if you don't want to, sweety," said K.

The little girl paused for a moment and then said, "Things weren't connecting right, is all." Then, looking at her father, she added, "But I fixed it. Didn't I, Daddy?"

"I guess you did, baby."

"And did you ever find the *cause* of the problem?" asked Samuel.

"No," said Lillie as she began to repeat the procedure with her fork.

"We tried to track it down the next day," added Adam. He winked at his daughter, who gave him a big smile. "We went up into the attic and explored all the electrical splices ...but couldn't find a short anywhere."

"That's not to say that there couldn't be something in the walls, he added. "We didn't break into the walls."

"Where a spider might have caused a short," said Donna as she eyed her husband and rolled her eyes.

"That's what an insurance agent told us years ago," she said. "This handsome young man from some insurance company came into our new apartment, sat us down, and did a hard sell on smoke detectors and an expensive insurance policy."

"Right," said Adam with a big smile. "Then he gave us a stuffed teddy bear dressed like a fireman and said, *'You know, a spider could cause a short and burn down your entire apartment complex just by shorting out a wire with its leg.*

"And you would be liable.'"

"Those guys are just so unscrupulous," said Samuel. "I remember when...."

"Lillie," K interrupted before her partner could start another lengthy story, "Is It true you can fly?"

Donna gave Dr. Paul an angry glare. "I thought we agreed that we weren't going to discuss...."

"We did," said K. "But Lillie is so forthcoming that I thought...."

And just then, Connie returned to their table with a trayful of drinks. She glanced from one customer to another and then began placing each beverage in front of the person who ordered it.

"Well done," said Samuel, giving the waitress an approving smile.

"Thank you, sir," said Connie. "Are we ready to order?"

"Just a few more minutes, please," said Dr. Paul. We haven't even looked at the menu."

"Take your time," said Connie and scurried away with her tray.

"Whee," said Lillie as she pulled her hands above her head and made a slaloming motion with her arms and body. "I'm flying," she said.

"Tell me about it," asked K.

"Can't," said Lillie. "Don't know how. "

But you jumped out of the top window of your home," said K. "Weren't you flying then?"

"Un uh," answered the little girl. And she raised her hand and moved it quickly from side to side in the air. "That's flying," she said.

Then she raised her hand again and slowly lowered it onto the table's surface. "That's gliding," said Lillie. "I can glide, but I don't know how to fly."

"And when will you learn?" said K.

"Don't know," said Lillie. "Maybe never. Maybe just my kids will."

"And who will teach them?" asked K.

The little girl shrugged, then picked up the menu and pulled it to her. Almost every item was described in both words and pictures.

"I'd like some of that," she said, pointing to a big, fat chili dog.

"Guess it is time to order," said Dr. Paul as he passed out the rest of the menus so his guests could order their lunch.

2

PARKER'S TRAGIC ROMANCE

Parker took Jason by the hand and led him to the door of her apartment. She reached into her pocket, took out the key, and pressed it slowly into the lock, but before she turned it, she faced him.

"Thank you," she said. "I had a wonderful time."

"So did I," he said, stepping toward her.

Parker pressed her hands against Jason's chest.

"And you were a perfect gentleman."

Jason glanced over at the apartment door, at the key all the way into the lock.

Parker read his look.

"Would you care to come in?"

He laughed.

*"Would I have to be a
perfect gentleman once
inside?"*

*Parker's eyes searched his.
Finally, she smiled.*

*"HELL NO!" she said,
throwing her arms around his
neck and kissing
him...passionately.*

K looked at Samuel as he drove back to Leland from Sacramento. He had that needy look in his eyes...the look of a writer who—despite his success—was terribly insecure about his work and desperate for approval.

"I think the new chapter is.... *interesting*," said K, hoping that Samuel would settle for an ambiguous comment.

"Thank you," he answered and then sighed, realizing it was all the praise he would get. "So, how's *your* writing coming?" he asked.

"I submitted my latest report last week. So, you'll have one on this adventure by end-of-day tomorrow."

"Of course, they're all safely filed on my computer and backed up onto the cloud. But what about the paper you're writing?"

"For the National Science Conference in Albuquerque?"

"Have you started it?"

K nodded and crossed her arms defensively. "I'm not too deep into it yet," she said. "But now that we've met with Lillie and her family, that's a lot more that I can add."

Sam shifted in his seat and looked out at the flat orchards of the Sacramento Valley as they rolled by. Then he turned back to K. "The kid is amazing,"

"And so sweet."

"And you still think it's a good idea?"

"To tell the scientific community about our research? YES."

"But people other than scientists read those papers once they're published."

"I know."

"Do you really want to tell the world that there's a new version of humanity popping up all over the country...probably all over the world? Kids who can control machines with their minds and maybe even FLY?"

"That hasn't happened yet," said K."

"I know," Sam answered, "but still...."

K's eyes brightened. "That reminds me, we've now found additional members of the angels in four different European countries and in Israel, Japan, and Korea. And, of course, there must be more."

"Great," said Sam with a mix of enthusiasm and dread. "I'm just saying it may be too early to tell the world about it."

"You know, a lot has to happen before my paper is accepted for presentation, let alone publication... all that vetting and peer review. So, it'll take at least another year."

"That may still be too soon," Sam grumbled. And it made K sigh in exasperation.

"Think about where these kids are popping up," she said. "We'll have to visit them in their home countries; we'll have to meet them, spend time with them. And some of them—like Melissa—will need relocation. Who's going to pay for all that? We'll need research support and government funding."

Samuel shook his head. "Of course. But what happens when some nut-job decides to kill off all the emerging angels while telling the world that it's for the good of humanity?"

"That could never happen."

Sam sighed, "If you publish that paper of yours, it probably will. And you know what could be even worse?"

K crossed her arms over her chest and felt a painful redness in her cheeks.

"You're going to tell me anyway," she said. "So go ahead."

"If somehow, some way," Samuel began, "word of your project is leaked to the media, and some hatemonger decides that it's just what he needs to stir up some shit...

"Then your kids and the rest of us will all be fucked."

NINE—BRAD DOCKSTER
(Sunset Studios, Hollywood, California)

1

Brad Dockster flipped off the microphone in the small audio booth. He'd just finished his daily broadcast, and now he gathered up his papers and sighed.

What was the use? he wondered.

Was anybody out there even listening anymore? Since the political games in Washington had died down, there didn't seem much interest in his kind of radio. The border conflict and climate change just didn't do it. His audience numbers were dwindling, and even those who were listening weren't really paying attention. He knew he had to come up with something new...a different angle, something to grab his audience. But what?

Dockster stood and pressed both hands into his back to squeeze out the nasty kinks he'd gained from sitting for almost two hours in a rigid, upright position. He was about to leave when his cell phone rang—as always—with the opening of The William Tell Overture.

Did he really want to answer? The caller was listed as UNKNOWN. Why bother?

On a whim, he decided to answer. What did he have to lose but his temper? So, he stuffed earbuds into each ear and tapped "answer."

"Brad here."

A raspy voice with a Southern accent and a menacing tone spoke softly through a very clear connection.

"Do you know who this is, boy?"

Brad recognized the voice immediately, and it thrilled and terrified him at the same time.

"Yes, sir, I do."

"How are your ratings, son?"

"They're good, sir. Very good."

"That's not what I see in my reports, son. I think they could be better."

Brad sighed—not audibly, he hoped. "Well, of course, sir, they *could* be better; they always can, you know."

There was a pause, then the raspy voice continued.

"You don't have much to talk about these days, do you?"

"Well, people still have a lot to worry about, sir. Climate change, China, Russia, the crisis at the border... threats to our way of life."

There was a pause on the line, and Dockster took the opportunity to move back to the studio chair. He spotted his coffee, reached for it, and took a sip. COLD...damn it.

"BULLSHIT," boomed the voice in the earbuds. "You got NOTHING to talk about, Brad. You're repeating the same useless crap every fucking day. No one cares."

"The elections are coming up, sir."

"Still a long way off... too far away, and who knows what will happen there anyway. What you need is something that will SCARE THE SHIT OUT OF EVERYONE, **RIGHT NOW**."

Dockster ran his fingers through his hair. Did he really need to be reminded of his troubles by this son of a bitch? He was ready to hang up. Except the dude WAS brilliant. Wasn't he? Everyone knew that... and dangerous.

"Of course, I'm always looking for new material," Brad said at last.

"Good, then," came the response, and then a series of loud coughs blasted through the earbuds, feeling like they would practically explode Dockster's head. But when they stopped, the voice managed to choke out very welcoming words, "I think I might have just the thing for you, boy."

"Really?"

"Can you get onto Google?"

"Sure."

Brad quickly called up Google on his phone.

"Check out Leland University...Research Faculty...Dr. Kathleen Kelly," said the raspy voice,

and, in seconds, Brad was staring at a rather academic-looking image of K.

"Cold but attractive," he said.

"She's much better looking than that," answered the voice. "But it's not the point. The fact is she's made an amazing discovery, one I think could be extremely useful in your broadcasts."

"I'd like to hear about it."

"Anyone else around there right now...anyone listening in?"

"I'm wearing my earbuds, sir," said Brad as he checked around the small studio to make sure that no one could be listening. "No one can hear you...no one seems to be in the building at all. So, tell me about it."

2

Half an hour later, Brad Dockster was out of the audio booth and pacing the studio floor. He had finished drinking the cold coffee and now began tearing the cup into little pieces, which he tossed haphazardly toward an ashtray sitting on the corner of the console.

"Let me get this straight," he said, "These kids don't have a part of the brain that we do, the one that makes us panic. So, they've no fight or flight instinct."

"That's it."

"And they can control machines with their minds, and their eyes can...what?"

There was a pause as though the person on the end of the line—in spite of the importance of the call—was getting very tired.

"They can look at you and scare the shit out of you... terrorize you with the way their eyes blaze."

"And you think we should alert the general public to these kids and let the world know the threat they pose?"

"Aren't we in danger, Brad? I mean, this is no slow, thousands-of-year process. This is an evolutionary *leap*. You've read about them. Evolution builds and builds unnoticed, and then one day, BAM! Thousands, maybe millions of members of a whole new species, suddenly show up and take over.

"And it's happening right now. No one knows how many of these kids there are or how old. There could be adult members of this species all over the world. The next Hitler could be about to pop up in China or Russia or Iran or Germany or Brazil and begin to lead them all in a quest for world domination."

"JEEZUS," said Dockster. "But wait. There's really no evidence how many of these kids there are, or if any of them are older than fifteen, or if they have any leadership skills, or want to dominate anything."

"SCREW YOUR HEAD ON STRAIGHT, WILL YOU, BRAD," the voice growled through Dockster's earbuds. "These kids have death-ray eyes, can run machines with their minds, and don't have the mental equipment to be afraid. If history tells us anything, it's that every new species REPLACES the old one. So, if we let these kids take over, we're screwed.

"I see, sir."

"YES! But that's where a man with your considerable talents can help, Brad. I'm willing to feed you all the details you need to get the word out. You can *dramatize* this threat to the listening public and bring it to life for them. WILL YOU DO IT?"

Dockster was glowing with pride at the position of honor this man seemed to place him in. "Of course," was his intended response, but as he often did, Dockster managed to come up with the wrong question.

"Will it improve my ratings?"

"WILL YOU GET YOUR HEAD OUT OF YOUR ASS?" screamed the voice on the phone. "The world as we know it is about to come to an end. Forget about climate change. Forget about the border, civil rights, and women's rights, and inalienable rights. THIS NEW SPECIES is the real threat...these kids! We have to save ourselves from them. So, are you with me on this or not, Brad?"

"Of course, I am, sir."

"All right then. I'll send you a series of fact sheets and guidelines that you can use to put your broadcasts together. You can't exactly ask people to go out and kill these kids...but you have to get your listeners so riled up that the threat will be crystal clear. Then what they do is up to them."

Dockster grinned. "Yes, sir. I'm eager and ready to help."

"All right then, I'll have my assistant call you with all the details. We want to keep you up to date on the latest developments."

"Yes, sir."

"You're a good man, Brad, and you may, in fact, help save humanity. Now, goodbye."

"Goodbye, sir."

Dockster pulled out his earbuds and threw them onto the console in front of him. Then, he fell to his knees and began shouting at the top of his lungs:

"THANK YOU, JESUS. THANK YOU! THANK YOU! THANK YOU!"

3

No more than a week later, as Samuel made his way onto the freeway heading toward work, he turned on his car radio and clicked over to News-Talk Radio.

"Time to listen to the crazies," he told K, who was riding in with him while her car was in the shop.

"Do we have to?" she asked.

"I think we have to know what we're up against," Sam said and turned up the volume on his least favorite shock jock...a guy he considered one of the most dangerous of them all.

> *Time for another edition of "THAT'S WHAT I THINK" from your friend, Brad Dockster, who ALWAYS tells it like it is. But first...*

K turned down the radio volume as some inane jingle came blasting through the old Mercedes speakers. "Not Brad Dockster," she begged. "Please, no."

"Time to face the music, K," Sam said with a nasty smile. "Know thine enemy."

"Don't you have a new chapter of your novel you want me to read?" K asked in desperation.

"Wish I did," said Samuel, "But I'm facing a little writer's block. Hopefully, it will pass. But in the meantime—as I often tell my PhD students, **"SHUT UP AND LISTEN."**

And just to prove a point, Samuel cranked the volume back up as Dockster's grating voice returned.

> ***Today's topic friends...***
> ***THE FUTURE... and guess***
> ***what... it doesn't just suck... it***
> ***doesn't even EXIST... not for***
> ***you and me anyway.***
> ***Pretty soon, folks...we're***
> ***not going to have a future***
> ***because we'll be***
> ***NOTHING...we won't count***
> ***any more.***

You see, way up there in Northern California, at Leland University ...which apparently is more than a football powerhouse, Dr. Kathleen Kelly, better known to her friends as K, claims she's found a whole new SPECIES of superhuman beings... one she likes so much she's calling them angels.

Dockster's entire tone suddenly changed as he chatted for a moment with his sidekick/engineer on the radio side.

By the way, have you seen Dr. K's picture, Tom? She is a looker—can I say that—this Dr. Kelly. A beautiful woman... long legs... terrific rack. But does she know what she's talking about? I don't think so.

Anyway, Kelly claims to have found— NOT just a bunch of angels who are going to swoop down, fight

140

*evildoers, and save our world.
Oh, no, friends. Because it
won't be OUR world
anymore. It will be theirs.*

*You see, Kelly's angels are
different from us...especially
their brains. They don't feel
fear. You could meet one on
the street, slap him across the
face, and he might just smile
and say thank you, while he
and his brothers and sisters
are dismantling human
civilization behind our backs.
Or he might disintegrate you
with his deadly ray-gun eyes.*

*That's right. These kids
have silver-glowing eyes
that—I'll bet—
can melt your face if they
want to. They can kill us, and
we won't have any way to
stop them.*

*I like to think evolution
takes thousands of years for
a new species to take over
the world. But suddenly, we
have this EVOLUTIONARY
LEAP...kind of a quantum leap
without the melodrama--and*

now we have this new species popping up everywhere...with powers we can't control... they want action now, believe me. They're not willing to wait. Soon they'll be marching on Washington, marching against us all, face-melting anyone who gets in their way.

Dr. K's angels don't care what's wrong with Planet Earth because they're going to fix it...for themselves. BUT NOT FOR US, remember that. We, apparently, are just in the way, so their plan is simply to TAKE OUR WORLD AWAY FROM US! FACE-MELT US ALL. <u>RIGHT NOW!</u>

"WHAT IS THIS?!" called Samuel as he instinctively hit the brakes causing his car to fishtail amid the commute traffic. Fortunately, he was able to bring the old Mercedes back under control without sideswiping any cars in the parallel lanes.

"Close call," he murmured.

Meanwhile, Dockster continued.

> *They're going to leave you and me out in the cold, left behind, soon to be extinct.*
>
> *Kelly's angels don't need us or our institutions, friends. They'll simply dismantle our schools, our businesses, our jobs, and our future. You know that upcoming raise you're worried about pal? Forget it! Pretty soon, there won't be any raises...in fact, you won't have a job and won't be able to get one either.*
>
> *Wonder about getting little Jimmy or Janey into a good school? What school? Pretty soon, there won't be any schools...this new species doesn't need schools... and if*

*they don't need something,
we won't have it either.*

*Are you worried about
your future? Hell, according
to Dr. K Kelly of Leland
University, you have no
future, your family has no
future, I have no future...none
of us do. These Killer-
Kidstrocities are coming after
us, and they're going to take
it all away.*

*Face-melting isn't their
only weapon, folks. Hell no!
According to my well-
connected undercover
sources, this new species of
kids can run equipment with
their minds. I mean, forget
the controls; their brains just
take over, and they can drive
a truck when they're not even
behind the wheel.*

*Some rumors suggest that
they can even fly—just launch
themselves from a window
and take right off.*

"My GOD," said K, "how could he

possibly know all this?"

"Sounds like he's got a mole in our research department," said Samuel. But then K shushed him so that they could hear the rest.

> **Dr. K Kelly isn't saying much about all this. She won't even talk to the press. And her boss—that grouchy old SOB, Samuel Wentworth—is even more defensive. That's why some HERO out there in the DOCKSTER NATION—some bright young mind who shall forever remain anonymous— found out about Dr. K Kelly and her research and told us all about it.**

"Fuckers!" cursed Sam through gritted teeth, and K could see that his hands were turning white from gripping the steering wheel so tightly.

Well, I say, stop hiding your beautiful body and curious mind under those academic robes, Dr. K. Come out, show yourself, and tell us what you've learned. If a new species is emerging—about to face-melt the human race into extinction—we want to know about it. AND WE WANT TO DO SOMETHING ABOUT IT.

Samuel glanced over at his partner and saw her eyes growing wide with anger.

"Misogynist asshole!!"

Do you know what I think? Dockster announced to

prerecorded cheers.

I think COUNTERATTACK!

We shouldn't give up without a fight! I mean, come on, we're the race of Julius Caesar, Napoleon Bonaparte, and Donald J. Trump? We're the good guys, remember.

So, let's find those little bastards—these Killer-Kidstrocities— round em up, and stick em on some desert island where they can evolve to their hearts' content...IN ISOLATION...FOREVER until they're the ones that DIE OUT.

SO—WARNING, Dr. K Kelly and all your strange new protégés: WE'RE COMING FOR YOU. And when we find you...it will be a serious form of GOODBYE!!

At least, THAT's WHAT I THINK!

And now a word from Tasty-Nut peanut butter.

PART TWO
HUMANITY FIRST

TEN—DEBBIE
(Sherman Oaks, California)

1

Debbie smiled happily. She twisted her long blond hair between her fingers and checked herself in the mirror. Her makeup was fresh, her hair washed, her teeth sparkly from that new kind of brightness treatment she was getting...whatever it was.

A freshly washed cotton blouse and jeans would be enough, she decided. Her husband had just called...telling her that he'd struck it rich... literally! Well, not today but tomorrow for sure. That's why he wanted her to run out and buy a new dress...the sexiest thing she could find because tonight they were going to celebrate.

Debbie gathered up her keys, her wallet, and her one-year-old baby and ran for the car... a well-worn old

BMW she and her husband bought secondhand some years ago. Maybe a new one was on the horizon.

"New dress...new dress...Mama's buying a new dress," Debbie sang as she rifled through the racks of clothes at REGINA DI BELLEZZA, the exclusive women's clothing store on Rodeo Drive.

"Mama buyin'—buyin'—buyin'," little Alex added.

The kid was cute...real cute, Debbie thought as she grabbed the sexiest outfit on the rack.

It was KILLER! Tight, short, with a VERY low neckline...PERFECT.

"Ohhh, baby-baby," Debbie sang as she handed the baby to the saleswoman, pressed the dress against her body, and tried some of her old college dance moves right in front of the mirror.

Very hot for a new mom, she thought. Then she spun around, did a little shimmy-shake, and suddenly noticed little Alex staring at her from the saleswoman's arms.

"Mmmmm, baba," the kid gurgled...or was Debbie just imagining it? She blushed and felt very embarrassed, but little Alex just kept smiling.

"Good boy," she said, grabbing the dress and ducking into the changing room to try it on. It looked perfect, and so did she. Her eyes were bright and excited, and her smile —finally, after years of bitter disappointment—was strong, happy, and positive.

Tonight, at Rocco's—their favorite Italian bistro— her husband would tell her all about his big success...the sale...the contract...the fantastic future he had only hinted at. She couldn't wait to buy the dress, go home, make herself luscious, advise the babysitter, take a taxi to Rocco's, and then...

2

"You'd have been so proud of me, Babe," her husband said as he did his best to 'go easy' on the martinis. This was going to be a beautiful night, and he didn't want to ruin it with too much alcohol.

"Tell me about it," Debbie cooed.

He waited for the server to bring their salads. Then—as his beautiful wife dug into the first really good meal she'd had in over a month—Brad Dockster leaned back, smiled, and told her.

"I'd just finished my broadcast," he began, "when I got this phone call from THE MAN."

"You mean…"

"Yeah, him. He's got this new angle…sensational…about these kids who have been identified by this science chick back at Leland University."

"Woman," Debbie corrected. "Woman scientist."

"Yeah, right. This woman scientist at Leland found a bunch of kids with different kinds of brains. They're more evolved than the rest of us, she says."

"How?" asked Debbie. "What are they?"

Brad shrugged. "I don't know how or what. It doesn't matter. The old man's point is that these kids are a threat to *our* kind of people...*our* way of life...*our* species."

Debbie's expression turned curious for a moment and then concerned. "What kind of threat?"

Brad kept grinning. "Like they've already evolved past us. They'll leave us in the dust, and we'll all soon go the way of the dinosaurs and Neanderthals."

Debbie's expression was blank. Apparently, she still didn't get it.

"You know. Neanderthals...they lived alongside our ancestors, the homo sapiens, and evolved with them. But we were better at getting along in the world, so they just died out. The way *we* will when this new species takes over."

"Well, fuck," said Debbie. It was the first time she'd used the "F" word since little Alex came into the world.

"It's okay, baby," Brad said. "I may have been embellishing a little. I mean...the business about Leland and the science gal is real, but you know, the old man wants me to turn it into entertainment...make a story out of it. And—guess what? I can do that."

Debbie grinned. Brad was the best storyteller she'd ever met...in a good way. It was one of the reasons she loved him.

"So, I took the guy's basic info, did a little more research on evolution, and came up with this."

He held up the front page of the _LOS ANGELES CHRONICLE._

The banner headline said,

FUTURE EXTINCTION? HOW WE CAN SAVE OURSELVES,

BY ALLAN ALLGOOD.

Debbie grinned at her husband. _"You're_ Allan Allgood?"

"Of course, I am, baby. He's the print and internet version of Brad Dockster. Only I can afford to be a little more intellectual in print. After all, this isn't radio, babe; _readers_ are naturally smarter than _listeners._"

"Is that right?"

"Abso-friggin-lutely! And I can present different points of view, really stir things up... build my following in print and on the web. For example, when the religious fundamentalists learn about this...What do you think *their* take will be?"

"Don't know," answered Debbie, still smiling with enthusiasm.

Dockster didn't answer... just continued right on.

"And what about other scientists...like maybe some think that this '*Woman* Scientist' doesn't know enough about evolution. I'm sure I can find some crackpot Ph.D. somewhere who'll argue the fine points with her.

"Hell, I can bounce all over the map...keep lighting fires...keep stirring shit up."

"And the *average* American?" Debbie asked.

"Dockster speaks to them, baby. Hopefully, Allan Allgood will be his intellectual half-brother, supporting my Dockster rants but adding depth for the *reading* public."

Brad turned then, grabbed his iPad, tapped the screen a few times, and held up an image of the front page of the LOS ANGELES CHRONICLE: electronic edition.

"They ran this yesterday with my story as the lead. The newspaper sold out in a few hours.

"Ed Feeney, you know—the editor—got so excited that he gave me an advance for four more articles... with more to come.

"His assistant is currently setting up podcasts for me; they want me to run them twice a week.

"If things work out, I'll get a permanent gig: regular salary, benefits, the whole nine yards."

Debbie's eyes grew even brighter.

"If it flies—and baby, it will believe me—we will be GOLDEN... RICH. The San Francisco Examiner and other major papers have already contacted the LA Chronicle, asking if they can run my articles. Feeney wants to syndicate me."

Debbie was thrilled but also concerned...gratified and yet worried.

"But what do you know about this stuff, Brad? I mean, really?"

"It's all storytelling, baby. It's make-believe. And way down deep, no one really cares. No one believes any of it. They just want a little excitement in their lives."

At this point, their waiter rolled a serving cart up to their table.

"Fillet mignon medium-rare for the lady," he said as he placed the entree in front of her.

"This is amazing," she said.

"Stick with me, girl," Brad cheered, "and I'll give you *'amazing'* every day. You deserve it."

And now a serving platter lowered in front of Brad.

"For the gentleman, the lobster tail."

Brad studied the spectacular entre with a hungry grin. Then he glanced across the table and watched Debbie's eyes tear up with gratitude. (And—by the way—had he also realized just how sexy that little dress looked on his wife? It sure brought back memories of their honeymoon in Ensenada.)

"I love you, Brad," she said.

"I told you I would take care of you and little Alex, didn't I?"

Debbie nodded.

"This is our ticket, honey. I'll keep telling my stories on the radio and now in print, and people will keep eating them up. I'm good at it. You know that. Don't you?"

Debbie bit her lip, reached across the table, and took her husband's hand. "Thank you, sweetheart," she said.

3

The first real protest against Dr. K's angels occurred only four days after Allan Allgood's (Brad Dockster's) second editorial appeared in the _Los Angeles Chronicle_. He had decided to riff on the concept of evolution itself, playing to religious conservatives. Not exactly denying the science, but challenging it by writing:

> *Dr. Kathleen Kelly and her supporters at Leland University, who rely so heavily on the theory of evolution to justify their assumptions about this new species, may not understand the theory as well as they think. There may be so much MORE to evolution than any of us know...or so much LESS. It is, after all, only a theory. So, here's another theory. Maybe these kids are really* monsters...*KILLER KIDSTROSITIES...direct creations of Satan himself, manufactured in the netherworld to challenge our faith and lead us into temptation and acts of evil. I think the theory that Satan created*

*these KILLER KIDS is as
plausible to God-fearing
Fundamentalists as
evolution is to non-
believers. Don't you?*

Seminal College, a small, ultra-right-wing divinity school in Utah, reprinted Allgood's editorial on the front page of its student newspaper, THE CALLING. The article was accompanied by an open invitation from the paper's editor and chief, Thomas Morton, asking all students to assemble and protest the protection and cultivation of satanic monsters at Leland University.

The college dean— Chatsworth P. Chatsworth D.D.—heartily endorsed the protest in an evening interview with the local Fox affiliate.

The next day, seventeen students marched through the campus's main quad, carrying placards reading EVOLUTION IS A MYTH and STOP PROTECTING KILLER KIDS.

Megan Morton, twin sister of the campus newspaper's editor, dressed in a grey wool skirt and ski

160

jacket, carried a large megaphone and repeatedly called out, "STOP INTERFERING WITH GOD'S PLAN," and "SCIENCE IS FOR DUMMIES."

When her brother saw the minivan with the CHANNEL 7 NEWS logo and the camera looking right at Megan, he rushed to her side and shook his fist IN SUPPORT. Megan raised the megaphone and continued shouting, "KILL THE MONSTROCITIES! KILL THEM ALL."

The camera zoomed back from the twins just enough to take in several of the other protestors and their signs but refrained from showing just how small the crowd actually was. Nor was the fact mentioned in the news broadcast that evening. It talked more about Allan Allgood's version of the supposed new species than about the protest itself. Still, the story was picked up by the network and distributed to all its affiliates with the headline:

PROTESTORS DECRY PROTECTING KILLER KIDS.

4

One week later, Brad Dockster did a seeming about-face in his third Allan Allgood editorial. Now interpreting the theory of evolution, he announced that the next evolutionary stage of humanity intended to destroy all of mankind to ensure its successful progression in the natural order.

"I don't get it," Debbie told Brad after reading his latest article.

"Of course, you don't, babe. No one does. It's just some science babble I threw together to stir things up out where the crazies live.

"Protests and rallies are what we need to keep this thing going."

Debbie smiled and shrugged. "Whatever pays the bills."

Brad nodded. "And believe me...when it comes to college protests, nobody does it better than UC Berkeley. They're a bitter rival of Leland, you know, and the world capital of student protests."

Brad's idea was dead on. Because, at that moment, members of the Tri-Omega Fraternity on the Berkeley campus were already preparing to respond to his latest editorial.

"Gotta stop those little fuckers," grumbled Frat President Carter Woodley in the basement of the Tri-Omega house. "Leland shouldn't be housing and protecting Killer Kids."

"I hear they're really the Spawn of Satan," said his pal, Harold Tryon, with a sneer.

"No, *you're* the Spawn of Satan," Carter responded.

"Oh yeah," answered Harold, turning his hands into claws and leering at the frat prez with a monstrous snarl.

Harold was a bulky kid, tall, with thick arms and thighs and a massive gut he liked to swing around in front of him when he walked. It played havoc with his balance and coordination, but it gave him a sense of who he was...HUGE HAROLD...the biggest guy in the frat, now squatting on the frat-house floor, nailing signs to poles.

The problem was that Harold wasn't much of a carpenter, missing the nail head on almost every other swing. He bent nails, smashing marks and deep gouges into the signs' faces.

"Never took a shop class in your life, did you, Harold?" teased Carter's girlfriend, Chang-Chang Woo. She wore torn jeans and a thin, cut-off t-shirt that exposed her slim waist.

Chang-Chang was using a thick brush to paint bright red slogans on the massive hunks of cardboard she'd propped up against the basement wall.

Blowing hair from her eyes with every brush stroke, she eventually finished, dropped the brush into the paint bucket, jumped up and down, gave a small cheer, and stepped back to admire her finished work. She'd made five massive signs, each with her own personal slogan, "EVOLUTION, MY ASS!"

"You *do* have a nice ass, baby," said Carter.

"Well, yeah? So do you," Chang-Chang answered, and she stepped up and grabbed his tight booty just to prove her point.

"Problem is," grumbled Huge Harold from down on his hands and knees, "if this new species is really the result of Natural Selection, then what the fuck are you doing painting a sign about your ass?"

Chang-Chang rolled her eyes. "Whatever," she said without letting go of her guy.

"Not whatever," answered Huge Harold. "That Leland bitch is trying to *influence* evolution, and that's not how it's supposed to work."

"What she's doing isn't science, anyway," said Carter. "It's just a bid for attention...a way to get more funding for a school that's already so filthy rich they don't know what to do with all their money."

"Wish they'd send some over here," said Chang-Chang. "I could use a trip to the Islands."

"Yeah, girl," added Carter, "You and me together on the beach...with the sunset, the surf, the mài tais."

"*Focus*, people," said Harold. "You guys can go tripping some other time. Right now, we have a species to save…OUR OWN."

And, with those words, Harold pushed himself onto his knees and then stood up quickly. He lost his balance and stumbled wildly in all directions, actually putting his foot through one sign before he caught the side of the couch and came to rest.

Chang-Chang had backed into a corner to get out of his way, but now she stepped forward.

"I'll get the signs for you," she said as she reached down and lifted one sign after another, handing them to the boys.

Then she grabbed one of her own signs and marched out the door, leaving Carter to follow her into the blazing California sun. Huge Harold came marching after them.

The three students passed their work on to other eager protesters and then joined in the chant, which was already starting, already being captured by five local and six international news agencies.

"STOP HIDING MONSTERS – STOP PROTECTING MONSTROCITIES!"

The protest was a huge success—as are almost all protests at Berkeley—with hundreds of students participating and complete news coverage from around the world. Of course, the campus police were too experienced to allow the event to get out of control...unlike so many of the other protests that followed.

ELEVEN—BOBBIE
(Department of Homeland Security— Washington, DC)

1

It was a dreary day in Washington, DC. Thick grey clouds sat right on the pavement, full of heavy drizzle and just enough wind to make things really uncomfortable. It was cold, too—in the mid-forties—that nasty time between fall and winter when it was too warm to dress for snow but too cold to do anything else.

Bobbie Jenkins stood in the middle of it all, smoking and cursing anything and everything...especially the fact that she had to stand outside to have a cigarette.

She looked down into a nearby puddle that reflected her image. "Getting fat, God damn it," she murmured. Bobbie knew it was beauty or donuts, and right now, the donuts, pizzas, and booze were winning.

She watched the breeze messing with the ugly, brown leaves that had long since lost their color and now just looked like shit...literally.

Bobbie had one hand in her suit coat pocket and the other on her cigarette, holding it away from her, studying the burning tip for a moment, then taking another drag. Right now, good old Camel cigarettes seemed to be her only friend.

"Hey, boss," came a cheery voice from behind her, and Bobbie turned to see the new guy, junior analyst Niles Powers, marching toward her. He smiled handsomely at a time when the last thing Bobbie needed was handsome. She felt sluggish and overweight and anything but beautiful.

"There was a time when..." she thought.

But that was a whole other story.

Niles was *a hunk,* though; tall, black, with the body of a guy who spent two hours in the gym every goddamn day.

"Hey, boss," he repeated.

"Hey, yourself."

"You wanted to see me?"

"Thought I said it could wait till I finished my cigarette."

"No need," said Niles. "I like it out here."

"Then you're a fucking idiot," said Bobbie as she reached into her pocket and pulled out a folded printout of an article from this morning's Washington Post... reprinted from the Los Angeles Chronicle.

"Seen this?" And she shook it open and held it up so Niles could read the title.

"Oh yeah. Who hasn't?" said Niles. "**Get rid of the Kidstrocities, say Berkeley Rioters.**"

"Just what we *don't* need with the country already divided over meaningless shit and the crazies taking over everything."

"I like your optimism," said Niles.

"I like your jacket."

Niles turned around slowly, showing off the waterproof slicker that neatly deflected the same drizzle soaking into Bobbie's wool coat. She shivered, and Niles gave her a sympathetic smile.

"So, a researcher at Leland," said Bobbie, "has identified several kids in the U.S. who have brains that are formed differently than the rest of ours. They have less, you know, lizard brains—less fight or flight response."

"Less unnecessary panic. No panic attacks."

"More confidence."

"A step farther removed from the reptiles we've all got hiding inside us."

"There's more," said Bobbie.

"You mean like the fact that some groups think they're a threat to the human race?"

Bobbie gave him a sour look and tossed her cigarette into the nearby storm drain.

"Something stupid like that."

"Or how about the conservative Christian point of view that scientists are using the false concept of evolution to make money and subjugate others...against God's will."

"We'll, yeah, there's that too," Bobbie said, looking at Niles with just a trace of admiration. "You do your homework, don't you?"

"I try," he said, flashing that handsome smile again. Damn, thought Bobbie. He even has dimples.

"What's likely," said Bobbie, "is that this is just another example of some ad guy inflating the truth to make a buck. I mean, the woman hasn't even presented her findings formally, and she's being quoted in every damn media source in the country."

"What does she *say* about it?" asked Niles.

"Nothing. A spokesman from the university says they are looking into the matter. Meanwhile, it looks like even more negative protests are on the horizon."

Bobbie turned and motioned toward the entrance. "Let's get out of this mess."

Niles followed her back into the warmth of the building. "You know, if you gave up smoking, you wouldn't be out in the muck every hour."

"Not a chance."

"And what are we going to do about all this anyway?" Niles asked. "Just wait until someone kills one of the kids?"

Bobbie turned and smiled.

"How's the weather at Leland?"

"Definitely better than this."

"Okay. Why don't you set up a meeting with Dr. Kathleen Kelly and her boss? I hear she has at least one member of this new "species" living on campus. Let's pay them a visit."

"To study the kid firsthand...warn her about the protests?"

"Absolutely," said Bobbie, "and to tell her how we plan to keep things from getting any worse."

2

Bobbie scrolled through the badly typed report on her computer screen.

She didn't especially like the twitchy old guy sitting across the desk from her. But he was a useful operative who said he had uncovered a dangerous new direction for THE PEACEKEEPING BROTHERHOOD.

"That's a supremacist group that began as a motorcycle gang but now cares more about politics than their machines," said Sonny Grabowski.

"So, you think the threat is real?" Bobbie asked.

"Now that all the other political crap has died down, yeah," he answered. "They have to find something to raise hell about, and this *species* thing is perfect."

Sonny had come into Bobbie's office wearing a leather jacket, jeans, and motorcycle boots. Probably his dressiest outfit, she decided. And now he sat there looking both angry and hopeful at the same time.

"So, they want to kidnap some of the new species kids?"

"Or just kill 'em," said Sonny. "That's what their leader, Josh Purdy, says. Says the kids aren't really human. They pose a threat to humanity, so they should be exterminated."

"Purdy doesn't know much about evolution, does he?" asked Bobbie.

Grabowski gave a shrug. Apparently, he didn't either.

Bobbie stood and walked around to the front of her desk, leaned against it, and stared at the biker. "So, what are you suggesting, Sonny?"

"Nothing, really."

"Bobbie crossed her arms, cocked her head, and waited.

"Okay. Maybe you guys should take the kids into *protective* custody."

Bobbie thought about the idea and then smiled. "You think Purdy and the rest of the Brotherhood would come after them if *we* were holding 'em?"

"Don't think so."

"So, it would be good for the kids?"

"Yeah."

"What about the kids in other countries?"

Sonny's eyes narrowed. "Oh…hadn't thought a that one. So, you think the Brotherhood might go after them too?"

Bobbie shrugged. "You tell me."

He considered the idea for a moment more and then shook his head. "NO!" Maybe Canada or Mexico, but realistically, 'NO.' Purdy doesn't like headin' outside good old American soil."

"So, all the more reason to protect those we have here."

"For their own good…and ours too, a course."

Bobbie nodded, and Sonny had to admit the reason he brought information to *her* instead of his other contacts. She could be a bitch, but she was damn intelligent and respectful.

"Good work," Bobbie said. And then, giving Sonny her warmest smile, she walked up to him, shook hands as he stood, and added, "Thanks, Sonny. This is just the kind of information I need to get things moving."

"In what way," asked the motorcycle cowboy spy.

"Just you watch," said Bobbie. "Just you watch."

TWELVE—ÁNGEL
(Outside Tucson, Arizona)

1

The pickup rumbled along the dirt road that skirted the northern edge of Rancho Rivera. Antonio was at the wheel with Ángel and his best friend Johnny Norris in the back seat. Antonio's grandson had recovered entirely from his accident, and now he and Johnny played video games on their phones while the old man drove along looking for signs of a massive brown bear reported to be on his property.

One of the ranch hands found two of his cattle torn to shreds by the beast, and the old man knew they had to track it down and get rid of it.

Sudden jumping and shouting in the back seat of the truck distracted Antonio.

"What the hell's going on?" he called.

"Video games," said Ángel as Johnny shouted, "GOTCHA!" Both boys began to squirm as the action of their play intensified. In his excitement, Johnny slammed his foot into the back of the front passenger seat, sending Antonio's lunch pail onto the floor. No harm done, the old man thought. It didn't open. Besides, the boys were engaged in a virtual shootout that he supposed might save the galaxy forever...or something like that.

Antonio laughed, glad he didn't have to listen to the explosions and wild music that accompanied the game. The boys heard it all through their earbuds.

"Mind if I turn on some talk radio," asked the old man.

Neither of the boys answered. They were deaf to the outside world.

"OKAY, IF THAT'S THE WAY YOU WANT IT!" shouted Antonio at the top of his voice, and he reached forward, turned up the car radio, and listened to the voice of the shock-jock in mid-broadcast.

*Do you know what I
think, said Brad
Dockster...*

  *New reports
suggest that this new
species of kids can FLY.
Can you believe it? I
mean, we already
know that they plan to
try and get rid of us,
our way of life, our
sacred institutions, our
jobs, our schools. So, I
say for our own good,
let's
save <u>ourselves,</u> and...*

Antonio flipped off the radio before Dockster could finish.

"Fucking asshole," said the old man, and then he glanced quickly over his shoulder and into the back seat to see whether or not the boys had noticed his language. They sat side by side, working their phones, apparently not listening to him at all.

"TAKE THAT, SCUMBAG!" yelled Johnny as his body swerved to the left. Ángel responded with a swing to the right, and they both began to jerk around so wildly that Antonio pulled the truck off the road and stopped.

There was silence then until Johnny murmured, "Can't talk to you now...sorry...gaming."

Ángel suddenly stiffened in his seat. He saw his grandfather looking back at them, and he grabbed Johnny by the arm and squeezed it.

"Shut up, man."

"It's just Talley," Johnny whispered.

"I know, but..." and he nodded to Antonio, who continued to stare at the boys.

"What's going on back there?" asked the old man.

"Just playin' video games," said Ángel.

The old man nodded. "But you're talking to Talley?"

"She's *so* hot," murmured Ángel.

"You mean Talley Antone, that cute little girl from the reservation...the one I did the portrait of?"

"Why would we be talking to her?" asked Johnny.

"I don't know," said the old man. "And *how* were you talking to her anyway?"

"Through my phone?" suggested Johnny.

"Earbuds," said Ángel at the same time.

"*While* you're playing video games?" asked Antonio. "You can do that?"

"Earbuds connected to the phone through the game?" said Johnny.

Both boys looked stunned for a moment as Antonio said, "Better get your stories straight, kids." And he turned around, started the engine, and began driving along the fencing again, doing his best to spot the bear that had taken his cattle.

Still, he'd glance into his rearview mirror every now and then to see what was going on in the back seat.

Both boys played with less energy now...less enthusiasm.

182

"Can't talk to you now, Talley," Johnny mumbled once. But that was all.

2

Talley Antone took a step backward when she saw Antonio Rivera marching across the parking lot toward the little store where she and her best friend, Sarah, had just purchased soft drinks.

"Hey, little girl," called Antonio.

"Hi, Mr. Artist," she said with a grin.

"Can I talk to you for a second?"

"Will you buy us some cookies?" asked Talley, showing the dimpled smile that Antonio thought was unstoppably cute.

"Love to," he said as he moved into the little storefront, took the pack of Oreos that Talley held out to him, grabbed a bottle of coke from the tub full of ice and soft drinks, and slapped a twenty-dollar bill on the counter.

The heavyset woman standing at the cash register made change but didn't give it back to the old man. Instead, she held onto it as she watched Ángel and Johnny march up behind Antonio and point to the tub of icy drinks.

"Sure, go ahead and grab a couple. What the hell," said Antonio, gesturing for the woman to add two more soft drinks to his tab.

"And a bag of chips," said Ángel.

"And a bag of chips," added Antonio. The woman just smirked and made change once again.

@@

"So, here's what I don't get," said the old man as he and the four kids sat around the weather-beaten picnic table behind the store. "You kids are communicating, but not through your phones."

All four kids nodded in agreement.

"So then...How?"

"I just kind of think it, and Talley hears it," said Johnny.

"But you said the words out loud, Johnny."

"Don't have to," the boy answered. "It's like I say the words out loud sometimes when I'm just thinking...like I move my lips when I'm reading."

"Most of us just think it, though," said Talley. "And the others get it."

"That's the way all you kids communicate?" asked Antonio.

Ángel shrugged. "Some of us do. Others—you know—can't."

"Who can and who can't?"

"About six kids around here, mostly our age, can communicate without phones or anything," said Talley as she squeezed a whole Oreo into her mouth.

"I can't, though," said Sarah, "and it makes me sad."

"So then, she's not really one of you?" asked the old man.

"No, I'm not," Sarah sighed, and tears began to form in her eyes.

"Of course, you are, girl," said Talley as she gave her friend a hug. "And you always will be."

Antonio watched the interaction for a moment, noticing how this new breed of human—as he liked to think of them—cared for others. And then he asked, "So what language do you kids communicate in?"

Johnny smiled and said, "We don't need a language. Could be Spanish could be English, or anything. It all sounds the same when we're doing it. But we all understand.

THIRTEEN—KATHLEEN
(Leland, California)

1

***MIDTOWN DESPERATION – BY S.
A.***

*Parker stared into Jason's soft
blue eyes.*

*He is so damn handsome, she
thought, so understanding. She
traced the edge of his jawline with
the tips of her fingers, loving the
rough stubble there.*

*She longed to kiss him again
and again...knowing that this was
the one person she wanted to
spend the rest of her life with, to
have his children, to cherish and
protect him forever.*

K finished reading the printout of Samuel's latest
chapter.

"Yeah, okay," she said unenthusiastically.

"That's all?" asked the old man as he peered anxiously out from behind his desktop computer.

"I guess. I mean, she's found the right guy, and she loves him, so, yeah. But you know—so what?"

"So what?" asked Samuel. "It's the point of the whole damn story."

K balled up the page she'd just read and threw it at her boss.

"Can we *not* do this now, please? There's just too damn much going on."

"Like all the protests and the news commentary...ninety percent of which is negative?"

"That doesn't matter?"

"It doesn't? It puts the lives of every member of the new species of kids in jeopardy—not to mention *our* lives. And you say *it doesn't matter*?"

K fell into the big easy chair in the corner of the office and leaned forward, looking absolutely miserable.

"Who could have done it, Sam...leaked my reports?"

"Just about anybody. Some intern somewhere in the university, some aide down in the lab who saw you testing Melissa, some hacker who found a way onto your desktop and your reports to me. Leland security is putting everyone who has anything to do with our operation through the mill, let me tell you. Hell, they may even withdraw our membership in the faculty club?"

"Are you serious?"

"NO! On that last point," said Samuel with an uncomfortable smile. "But on all the others—YES."

"The internet chatter is really causing concern. And now with this new business about *clusters*."

Samuel stood slowly and walked to the chair where K was sitting. He took both her hands and held them for a moment, his eyes full of sympathy and yet curiosity.

"Tell me about the clusters again?"

"There have been reports from my colleagues overseas," K began. "When they do random testing of the kids surrounding the ones they've identified as

Angels, they find others with the same physiology. Apparently, they usually appear in groups."

Samuel nodded, took a deep breath, and let it out slowly, sounding almost like a low, desperate whistle. "Are any clusters showing up with the children we've identified?"

"One set. Remember Ángel?"

"The boy on the ranch in Arizona?"

"Yes. He has a close friend named Johnny Norris, an Indian kid who lives on the nearby reservation."

"So, no possible genetic relationship to Angel?"

"None. But the physiology of their brains is remarkably similar."

"Johnny hasn't been controlling equipment or machinery with his mind, has he?"

"Not that I know of."

"And no flying or swooping, whatever they call it?"

K smiled. "That would be floating, Sam."

"Sure, of course."

"Don't know," said K. 'But there are six other kids on that reservation who have the same kind of brain."

"Did they do random testing there, too?" asked Samuel.

"After they discovered that the kids were telepathic."

"What?"

"Yeah, they can talk to each other with their minds. Ángel's grandfather, Antonio, saw it happening. The kids know and trust him, so they told him all about it."

"Jesus," said Samuel. "What next?"

K shook her head. "Don't know. Anyway, breakfast tomorrow at the faculty club...that visit from Homeland Security, remember?"

Sam stiffened.

"Seven thirty AM."

"In response to the protests."

"Yeah."

"At least the Christian Right hasn't threatened to kill anyone," said K.

"Yet," added Sam, shaking his head. "But I'm sure that's a possibility the Homeland folks will want to talk about."

K stood, patted her boss on the shoulder, and moved to the door. "I'm going to turn in early. Busy day tomorrow. How about you?"

The old man shuffled back behind his desk.

"Nah. I'm going to spend a little time with my girlfriend. It's the most relaxing thing I can think of."

K laughed, "I thought *I* was your girlfriend."

"Sorry," said Sam with a sad smile. "You've been replaced."

"By whom?"

"Parker, of course," said Sam as he typed in his password, called up the manuscript, and started typing.

2

The Leland Faculty Club was set in a wooded area in the back corner of the campus. Branches from surrounding trees seemed to be trying to peer in through every window.

Inside, small freestanding tables stood far enough apart to allow privacy in every conversation. K and Samuel were already seated and sipping coffee when special agents Bobbie Jenkins and Niles Powers approached the maître d'.

The young man greeted them warmly, gestured to the two researchers, and led the agents to them.

K and Samuel stood, shook hands, and everyone found a seat.

"I trust you had a pleasant trip," said Sam.

Bobbie smiled as she waited for the server to pour some coffee and then took a quick sip.

"The plane ride was bumpy as hell," she said. "But it doesn't matter because your weather more than makes up for it. We left nothing but grey skies and slush."

K smiled. "We've been very fortunate this year. It's been in the 70s all month."

"I could get *very* used to that," said Bobbie.

"Yeah. That's the problem," said K. "You get used to it, and then you can't live anywhere else."

Bobbie reached for her menu as she saw the waiter approaching. She guessed he was probably a college student with enough experience to land a job in the prestigious university dining room.

"May I take your order?"

Bobbie spoke up. "Three eggs scrambled easy, bacon, and toast."

"Me too," added Niles. "But just one egg."

"Oatmeal, for me," said K.

"Double stack of pancakes," said Samuel, "sausages, syrup, and extra butter."

Niles winced at the older man's selection but refrained from commenting as the waiter repeated everyone's order. "Coming right up," he concluded and then headed back toward the kitchen.

Before he was even out of earshot, Bobbie turned to K and said, "How the fuck did you let someone get their hands on such *volatile* research? Why didn't you check with us first?"

K recoiled. She didn't expect the feds to lead with a personal attack.

"I didn't know I had to clear my research with the federal government," she said. "And we don't know who hacked my computer or how. It's protected in every way the university has."

"Well, you should have done better," Bobbie growled. "Ideas like those should have been treated with the secrecy you'd give the codes to the nuclear warheads."

"Highly classified," added Niles.

"Hey...hey...." responded K, holding up her hands as though blocking a punch. "It's important information that the scientific community needs to know."

"Is that why you came here, Agent Jenkins," asked Samuel, "to read us the riot act because someone leaked K's research?"

Bobbie took a deep breath, drew back, and finally seemed to settle down. Her posture relaxed. Her smile tried to return.

"Sorry," she said. "It's just that Niles, I, and a growing team at Homeland Security have to figure out how to deal with the aftermath of your little leak."

"It was a...." K began, but Samuel squeezed her arm, stopping her. "What aftermath?" he asked.

"Well, you've seen the protests for openers," said Bobbie. "They're starting to spread throughout the world. And we already have intelligence suggesting that several hate groups will try to kill the kids."

"Hadn't heard that."

Samuel glanced over at K nervously. "Serious threats?"

"Nothing in writing," said Niles, but some of our best agents have reported those kinds of conversations going on among white supremacists."

"Let's cut to the chase," said Bobbie. "Our office feels the safest action now is for the government to gather up the children you've identified and take them into protective custody."

"Like moving them into a little retreat," added Niles.

"But what if the kids or their parents don't want that?" said Samuel.

Gesturing toward K, Bobbie responded, "She should have thought of that before she got so damn candy-assed about protecting her data."

K shook her head. "THE PROBLEM is that these kids have talents none of us understand yet. They're brilliant, and there are more than a handful of them. Clusters are appearing all over the country, maybe thousands worldwide. Scientists everywhere need to know about them."

"And bringing them together into a single location," Samuel added, "will be difficult and—even if you can pull it off—you'll just be making them an easier target for the crazies."

"We have to protect them," said Bobbie, growing more aggressive as the conversation continued.

"If you want to think about protection," said Samuel, "your best bet is to deal with the hunters, not the prey. The prey may be very well able to take care of themselves...though I'm not sure how that will affect the rest of us *lesser* species."

"These kids can communicate telepathically...over great distances," said K. "They all have advanced intelligence. They can control machinery with their minds and are better suited to this world than we are."

Bobbie was about to respond when the waiter arrived with their breakfast.

"Scramble here," he said, placing Bobbie's plate in front of her. And the food looked so good, and she was so hungry that Special Agent Bobbie Jenkins decided to just eat.

"We'll talk more about the government's plans to take custody of these kids after breakfast," she said.

And then she dug into her bacon and eggs.

CHAPTER FOURTEEN— MELISSA

(Leland, California)

1

Dr. Kathleen Kelly and Melissa Washington walked across the main quad of the Leland campus, over the well-worn tiles in front of the non-denominational (though clearly Christian) church with its massive mural of the Sermon On The Mount.

Melissa studied the portrait of Jesus for a long moment, then turned and smiled at K as they walked through the porticos along the classrooms.

She looked up at the bright November sunshine and squinted, then turning to K, she said, "Not sure what I think about it. I mean, we have all been communicating lately, so I *can* ask the others. And I do love it here—you know. My mom and brother are so happy."

"Then what bothers you?" K asked.

Melissa wore cut-off Levi's and a simple Leland football jersey, neither heavy enough for the fifty-five-degree Northern California fall weather. But then, compared to Rochester, New York, in November, maybe shorts and a t-shirt *were* comfortable enough for the teen, K thought.

Melissa stopped, looked up at K, then into the sun, and squinted even more.

"Something just doesn't feel right," she began. "Feels like some kind of a trap. We can sense those, you know."

"I'm sure you can," said K. "Come sit down." And she led the girl to a bench in the warming sunshine.

"So, the idea of moving to Washington DC, into a supervised retreat run by the government scares you?"

"Yes."

"And will it scare the others?"

"I'm sure."

K crossed her legs toward the girl and smiled sympathetically. "Then how about this...housing right here on the Leland Campus...brand new housing built for you and your family?"

"Who'd run it?"

"I'd be in charge," K said.

Melissa's smile was sudden and immediate.

"Sounds so cool," she said. "I could see what the others think. But I bet they would like it. I would, for sure."

2

"What do they think?" Samuel asked as K entered his office.

"That would be a big 'NO' from Melissa on housing in Washington, but a very big 'YES' on moving to a permanent facility here on campus."

"And can she tell how the others feel about it?"

"Sure," said K as she went to the easy chair in the corner of the room and sat there fully upright...totally engaged despite the chair's seductive softness.

"She ran a little thought cycle while I was with her in the student union."

"No one noticed?"

"No, actually, nothing special happens when these kids communicate. They just seem to be doing something else, in our case, having a couple of hot dogs."

"Hot dogs? Okay."

"She took a little poll. The kids in Arizona were okay with coming here...all of them. Lillie, of course, didn't want to leave her family. So, that's something we'll have to deal with down the line."

"Yeah, we will," answered Sam. "And it may not be easy...I mean, maybe this isn't such a good idea."

"Scientists from one species trying to interfere with the evolution of another?" asked K.

"Shit," said Samuel, "we do it all the time. You know...wolves into dogs?"

"That worked out for us."

"Have you asked a wolf about it," Sam asked with a grunt, "...or even a dog?"

"Well, going back to good old Darwin," said Samuel, "the primary law is survival of the fittest. So, if these kids are to play out their destiny, they should be able to overcome the scientific crap we throw at them."

"Or that the government imposes. You know, supposedly for their own good."

K's look was suddenly very troubled, "Anyway, we have a Zoom meeting with Homeland Security tomorrow morning to talk about it."

Sam shuddered as he thought about the prospects.

"I know," K said. "I need to not think about it for a while. Need to clear my head."

"Really???" asked Sam, and there was a sudden brightness in his eyes as he came around to the front of the desk. "Then I have just the thing for you, Miss." And he handed K two stapled sheets of paper.

"Don't tell me...."

"You said you needed a distraction, and this should do the job."

Shaking her head, K took the papers," "All right. Why the hell not," she said as she leaned back in the easy chair and began to read.

MIDTOWN DESPERATION – BY S. A.

Parker felt the warmth of the silk sheets before she opened her eyes. And there he was...the beautiful man she'd spent the night with.... So close. He reached out, cupped her face in his hand, and a tingle moved all through her, all the way to the very tips of her toes.

"Morning, beautiful," he murmured.

Parker bit her lip and knew she had to say it.

"Morning," she answered, and then—yes,

she decided, she WOULD tell him.

"I love you, you know," she whispered so softly that she wasn't sure he heard her.

But he did.

His eyes grew dark. His jaw set, and—after a moment—he pulled away from her, turned his back, and got up from the bed.

"Wait...NO!... I didn't..." she began. But it didn't matter; he was gone.

Parker rose, went into the bathroom, and showered. She brushed her teeth, dried, and brushed her hair. She put on the fresh clothing she had laid out for herself the night before. But when she walked into the hallway, she saw that the door to

*his study was closed. Her
coat and bag were sitting
on a chair near the
entryway.*

*"NO!" she called in
sudden panic.*

*She went to Jason's
study and tapped lightly
on the door.*

*"Hey, wait. Can't we at
least talk about this?"*

*There was no sound at
all, and then—after a long
moment—a bitter roar,
"GOODBYE!"*

"Jesus, Samuel," said K. "I didn't expect that."

"No story without conflict," he said with an almost
evil grin. "You feel indifferent now?"

"But couldn't he just be on Parker's side and help
her through some difficulties...ones that they could face
together?"

"The deeper the conflict, the better the story," Sam
answered.

"If you say so, Mr. Best-selling Romance Novelist," said K as she got to her feet and handed the papers back to Sam.

"Anyway, thanks for that little _break?!_" she said, rolling her eyes.

"I thought you'd like it," Sam answered.

"Not exactly," K continued. "Anyway, gotta go. Gotta put together a plan to contact the kids. We'll need to reach out to them individually, but it sounds encouraging."

"Sure."

"And can I contact some of the new kids we've heard about?"

"How would our friends at Homeland Security feel about that?"

"Food for our Zoom meeting tomorrow," K said.

"Sure," Sam answered. "Just keep everything quiet. I don't want the crazies to have a head start on any of this."

"Yes, sir!" K gave the old man her best salute. "Will do."

But they both knew that the crazies already had a head start on everything.

FIFTEEN—BRAD DOCKSTER

(Los Angeles, California)

1

Brad Dockster walked into the office of Ed Feeney,
Editor-in-chief of the Los Angeles Chronicle.

"Feelin' good about everything today, boss?" Brad
asked.

"Never…. ever…ever," Feeney growled.

"Well, you will when you see this," said Dockster,
and he slid an image across the editor's desk. Feeney
picked it up and studied it. "And what the hell is this?"

He turned it sideways, upside down, even flipped it
over to the blank side. "I get nothin'."

Dockster smiled as he leaned forward over the desk.
"It's that kid, Ángel…one of the—you know—
Monstrosities. A friend of mine took it out in Arizona
with a drone camera, an extreme longshot, of course."

"So extreme no one knows what it is," growled Feeney.

"Yeah, I know," said Brad, tossing another image onto the editor's desk. "So, I blew it up."

"Still doesn't look like much."

Dockster smiled, "So, I enhanced it." And now he tossed a third print onto the desk. This one showed a clear image of a pre-teen boy, but his eyes were darkened...by the enlargement, but also by the hand of a skilled Photoshop artist. Teeth that had also been distorted into seeming crooked now were fanglike.

The editor laughed as he studied it. "Yep. There's our monstrosity, Brad."

"Like it?"

"Oh, I do. Do you have some copy to go with it?"

Dockster pulled a folded sheet of handwritten copy from his pocket and handed it to Feeney, who read it out loud.

"Okay, let's see, 'THE ENEMY!' he said as he read the headline. "I like that."

"Read on, chief," said Brad. And the editor did.

> "This is what we're up against...the monstrosities who want to replace us here on earth. When they're with us, they seem like normal kids, but get them alone—as this enlarged and enhanced drone photograph reveals—and these kids show what they really are...predators come to scavenge off humanity, destroy our families, and our way of life...and drive us out of existence."

"Excellent," shouted Feeney as he stood, came around in front of the desk, and clapped Brad on the shoulder. "Every newspaper in the country will want this on their front page."

"Just between you and me, I did take a few editorial liberties with..." Brad began.

"Who gives a shit," growled Feeney. "We're in the business of selling papers, aren't we? Issues of journalistic integrity flew out the window in the '90s. It's a new world, boy. Embrace it."

2
(Aswidth, Texas)

Police said they were ready to confront the crowd that called themselves the "Pro-Humanity Brotherhood." They assembled on the steps of Crowe Plaza on the campus of Aswidth State University in Aswidth, Texas, just two days after Allan Allgood's headline and picture, THE ENEMY, appeared in half the newspapers and all the internet news sources in America.

But what police captain Andy Rechsteiner thought would be less than a hundred student protestors had now swollen to nearly a thousand students joined by additional protestors from various groups, including students from the nearby divinity school, a large group of white supremacists, and members of a well-known motorcycle gang. They all clustered at the top of the steps at Crowe Plaza.

"Spread out," Rechsteiner told this cadre of campus security officers and local police. "Have your tasers ready, but don't draw, don't shoot, just march slowly up the steps using your shields to push the protestors out of the plaza.

Andy stepped in front of his troops, looked up at the sea of angry faces—as many old and grizzled as young and idealistic—and raised his megaphone.

"THIS IS AN ILLEGAL ASSEMBLY," he called. "YOU'RE BREAKING THE LAW. DISBERSE.

DO YOU HEAR ME? DISBERSE."

In response, the protestors carrying an assortment of signs that read HUMANITY FIRST, THE FUTURE IS WHITE, and REVELATION NOT EVOLUTION began chanting, "SAVE HUMANITY, SAVE OUR LIVES. SAVE HUMANITY, SAVE OUR LIVES."

Ignoring the chant, the police and security officers moved slowly up the steps. The front row carried shields, but their weapons were not drawn.

"Be prudent," Andy told his troops, and then he again called out to the protesters through the megaphone.

"WE DON'T WANT ANYONE TO GET HURT. DISPERSE!

"WE DON'T WANT TO HURT ANYONE. PLEASE LEAVE THE PREMISES."

As the first row of security officers reached the top of the steps, Charlie Manual, a fifth-year Ag student, suddenly hurled an unopened can of beer at one of the officers, striking him on the side of the head and dropping him to his knees.

The police around the injured man caught him, pulled him off to the side, and then charged the students, shields raised.

"FASCIST PIGS!" screamed Joanie Ridgeway, a young woman in the front of the crowd. And, taking a rock handed to her by another protestor, she heaved it at an oncoming policeman. The officer at the center of the advance tried to swat it away. Still, the rock was bigger than he anticipated. It slammed into his wrist, spinning him around and sending him tripping into the other security officers advancing up the steps behind him.

"SELLOUT," called Joanie bitterly, and the officer got to his feet, pulled out his nightstick, and charged.

Joanie's scream drew the attention of several television cameras covering the protest for local, national, and international media. So, a dozen cameras zoomed in on the action as the girl turned to run just as the officer knocked her feet out from under her and struck her across the shoulders with his club.

By then, many members of the crowd had dropped to their knees, holding their hands above their heads in peaceful protest. But others charged the security detail, pounding into them from the steps above, knocking them backward, and sending them spilling onto those behind them.

In response, several officers drew their guns and pointed them at the crowd. This forced more protestors to their knees while others turned and ran from the plaza.

But now, a large group of students began shouting at the officers.

Tim Morgan, captain of the university football team and straight-A student in Agribusiness, grabbed the lid from a nearby trash can and rushed directly into the crowd.

"WE DON'T WANT MONSTROSITIES HERE IN TEXAS!" he shouted as he began using the lid as a weapon, swinging it back and forth wildly, knocking over protestors and police in the process. Tim's advance drew other team members to him. Some attacked the police, sending Ross Jenkins, the newest recruit on the police force, toppling into a flank of his fellow officers.

Staggering to his feet, Ross pulled his gun and began shooting, first into the air but then at the students.

He hit Andrea Rodrigues, a young pregnant woman who had simply attended the protest to be with her friends.

Andrea fell and was nearly trampled in the melee of students fleeing the shooting.

Somehow, Charlie Manual, the science student who had thrown the beer can that started all the violence, saw Andrea fall, rushed to her, and pulled her away from the mob that suddenly attacked the police on the spot where she had fallen. He saved her life while protestors continued throwing rocks, the security forces continued shooting, and people on both sides of the protest began to die.

SIXTEEN—ÁNGEL
(Outside Tucson, Arizona)

1

Donny and Emma Minson had just celebrated their wedding...the most wonderful day of their lives. Sweethearts all through high school, Donny had proposed at the senior ball, getting down on one knee in the middle of the gym as other couples swayed to the music and the sound system sang out,

> I promise to spend my whole life through...
> ALWAYS BEING IN LOVE WITH YOU.

Then, Donny pulled a ring from his pocket and presented it to his sweetheart. Of course, Emma accepted. They were, in fact, the king and queen of the ball...probably the most popular kids in school.

Donny was president of the student council, editor of the school newspaper, and the best wide receiver on the school football team.

Emma was secretary of the council, star pitcher on the school's softball team, occasional cheerleader, and President of the student gun club. After all, she was a crack shot...so well trained by her father that she had won THE BULLSEYE AWARD for Best Teenage Target Rifle Shooter three years in a row.

Donny and Emma's romance started in the seventh grade when Emma told her girlfriends at one slumber party that she only loved two things in all the world... Donny and her Winchester rifle.

Best crack shot in Saint Louis County," read the plaque above the desk in the corner of Emma's room...right above Donny's eighth-grade graduation picture.

Donny had made a vow of pre-marital chastity at a Bible study ceremony that same year. But that vow and the one at his wedding were not the only vows he made.

In a Ritual of Manhood, a week before the wedding, Donny's father, Will, and several local lodge members had decided that they would all make another promise.

The lodge was a full-fledged subscriber to the Brad Dockster Inspired ***Humanity First Alliance***. As such, the Minsons and other lodge members vowed to protect mankind by searching out and destroying this new species of humanity.

Emma Minson wasn't an official lodge member, but she might as well have been. Because—in her heart— she made the same vow and enthusiastically agreed that their honeymoon would be a pilgrimage to at least one state where members of the new species had been spotted.

The Humanity First Alliance had published a list of the known Monstrosities and their locations. It was all in a little pamphlet entitled *WHERE THE MONSTERS LURK*. And so, two days after their wedding, Emma and Danny put on the new hunting gear Emma's dad gave them as a wedding gift.

Donny couldn't be more in love with his cute teenage wife, he realized. Somehow, she even looked sexy in camo gear, stalker pants, and hunting boots. Of course, Emma wasn't literally a teen, having just turned twenty, two days before the wedding. But she looked like an enthusiastic kid carrying her brand new.243 Winchester rifle...a wedding gift from Donny and perfect for a crack shot like his new wife.

The couple had flown into Tucson right after their small wedding reception, spent their honeymoon night in a modest suite at the local Travel Lodge, then woke up early the following day and drove out into the country.

Donny pulled over to the side of the road and parked their rental car in a spot noted in their guidebook, *WHERE THE MONSTERS LURK*.

"I'm sure you'll see a couple of them out there," the Reverend Jackson Smallet told Donny as they left their wedding reception. "Look for a clear shot, Son, and God will guide your hand."

The fresh mountain air felt chilly and invigorating, and the snow-covered crest of the Tucson Mountains beckoned to the couple as a formation of geese winged their way across the sky.

"Look-et there," called Donny.

"A sign of God's approval," added Emma, "pointing our way."

Donny raised his rifle to shoot one of the geese, but Emma reached up and quickly pulled his gun down.

"Not our mission, baby," she said. And so, Donny took a deep breath, turned toward his new wife, and stepped toward her.

"I love you so much," he sighed as they melted into their first long kiss since breakfast. Then Emma stepped back. Looked into his eyes and called out, "But let's get crackin', Babe. We got a mission, remember?"

And so, Donny led his pretty young wife up onto the ridgetop.

2

An old man and two boys hiked the fence line, checking the wire.

"Lookin' really good here," said Antonio Rivera as he grabbed the barbed wire with his gloved hand and pulled on it to make sure it was taught.

Ángel dropped to his knees to inspect the security of the lower fence. "Fine here," he said.

"Good over here, too," added Johnny Norris. The boy had come from the reservation to help his friend's grandfather inspect the fences along the back of his property.

"I'm thinking the place is safe for another few months anyway," said Antonio, and he pulled a bottle of water from his pack and tossed it to Ángel. The boy caught it, took a deep swallow, and passed the bottle to his pal.

"Hard workin' ranchers," said Donny Minson as he watched the interaction from across the valley.

Emma laughed. "Too bad that isn't *all* they are," she said as she raised her Winchester, aimed, and fired.

There was that classic snap from the gun, and one of the boys fell immediately beside the fence. Donny's shot dropped the second.

"Got 'em both," he said with a satisfied smile.

"Monstrosities," said Emma with a noticeable shudder. Then she turned, gave her new husband a high five, and shouldered her rife.

"Let's clear out of here," said Donny. "Not sure everyone will be in sync with our mission."

"They should be, though," said Emma. "Someday, the whole world will thank us."

"Yeah, we'll be heroes...husband and wife."

"Maybe even saints," the girl added, and together, the young honeymoon couple moved slowly back down the slope to their waiting car, happy to report their mission's success to the lodge members back home.

Meanwhile, across the valley, Antonio looked with horror at Ángel and his friend. He could see that Johnny, the younger of the two boys, was already dead, nailed right through the heart by an excellent shot.

Ángel seemed to be clinging to life, eyes closed, blood bubbling up through his lips and nose as he clutched his chest.

"Jesus Christ," called Antonio as he reached for his cell to call 911. But he didn't have to make the call. A medical helicopter was already on its way...sent from God knows where... contacted by God alone knew whom.

3

As they drove away from the mountains, their mission accomplished, Donny Minson noticed that it was 7:00 AM—right on the hour. So, he reached down and turned on the radio.

"If we're lucky, we'll be just in time," he told his pretty young bride.

"Oh, I hope so," she answered.

And yes! There he was...in crystal clear reception over the local airwaves, everyone's favorite shock jock...BRAD DOCKSTER.

Time for another edition of "THAT'S WHAT I THINK" from your friend, Brad Dockster, who ALWAYS tells it like it is. But first...

"Turn it up, babe," called Emma, and her new husband did. He wanted to hear their hero as much as she did.

Today's topic, friends, Let's Get Rid of The Monstrosities.

I'm calling on every red-blooded American to demand that we get rid of these monstrosities, these

*evolutionary anomalies.
Round 'em up, lock 'em
up, and throw away the
key.*

*I'm not advocating
violence against them
(chuckle), not me. I'm not
saying blow their damn
brains out. Do you hear
me? But let's end this sick
sideshow once and for
all.*

*I'm certainly happy to do
my part. And if there are
accidents, if somehow, as
the result of some tussle,
one of those Kidstrocities
dies... well, I'm not saying
'so much the better,' but I
am saying 'God's Will,
friends...all to the good'.
And if YOU happen to,
shall we say, help
deactivate one of these
Monstrosities, send me*

some evidence—a little write-up you do yourself, a photo or a newspaper headline, or any proof you have that you're the hero— and I'll send you a BRAD DOCKSTER HERO T-SHIRT absolutely free!! Strictly on the QT, of course.

And here's some related good news. One of my supporting senators— who prefers to remain nameless for now—has just introduced a bill in Congress declaring these monstrosities SUBHUMAN. He's got all kinds of scientific evidence and science experts to back him up, too.

Now, friends, doesn't that sound just about

right? The senator calls these kids an <u>endangering</u> species, got that...'endanger—ing' as in they are endangering US. They're a threat to humanity, one that should be eliminated.

The senator doesn't say how, of course. But I'm thinking he's seeking to declare <u>open season</u> on these Kidstrocities...putting them in a class with rabid dogs and killer bears.

Let's just hope there are enough reasonable members of congress to agree with the senator and pass his legislation.

"Did you hear that, Deb?" asked Donny. "We're safe...I knew we were. And we can get those HERO T-SHIRTS TOO...one for each of us."

"But we have no proof that we're responsible for today's action, honey," said Emma.

"Sure, we do. We have the plane tickets and pictures with our guns, and I grabbed a shot across the valley with my phone as the old man leaned over those monsters out there in the field. That should do it. DOCKSTER will keep our secret, save us from any assault charges or any Monster Protectin' Perverts out there."

"Oh, I'm so excited!" said Emma. And she reached across the console and gave the bulging muscles in her husband's right arm an encouraging squeeze.

Donny glanced at his wife and couldn't miss the eager expression in her eyes.

"Time to make a baby?" he asked.

She nodded, "As soon as we get back to the hotel room."

But Donny didn't wait. He jerked the car across two lanes of traffic and into an overlook at the side of the road.

Pushing her seat back as far as it would go, Emma welcomed her husband to her side of the car so that they could do what all newlyweds do...but very seldom in cars these days.

That's right, Donny and Emma re-consummated their marriage to the ongoing electric rant of Brad Dockster, who continued to call for the extermination of those Kidstrocities "for the good of humanity and the greater glory of our beloved land and our Lord and Savior. Amen."

And now a word from Tasty-Nut peanut butter.

CHAPTER SEVENTEEN—LILLIE
(Felicity California—Northern Sierra Foothills)

1

Lillie Allonzo had been on her hands and knees on the back deck of her parent's home, playing with her dolls, serving tea to Mr. Rumple, her teddy bear, and Baby Amelia. Now, she dropped the teapot, suddenly stared into space, listening to a thought conversation, and then answering politely, "Thank you." But the little girl was severely shaken by what she'd heard. She turned to her teddy bear, clutched him to her, and stood frozen in place for perhaps fifteen minutes.

Lillie's mother, Donna, found the little girl on the deck and thought for a moment that her daughter had suffered some kind of stroke. She moved quickly to Lillie, grabbed her by the shoulders, and shook her.

"Wake up, baby," she called. She raised her hand and was about to strike her daughter when Lillie turned her vacant eyes to her.

"They're killing us, Mommy!" she said. "One of us is already dead...maybe more. They're coming after me too!"

"Oh, no, baby," Donna said, falling to her knees and pulling the little girl to her.

"It's not true. You're all right. Everyone loves you. Nobody wants to hurt you."

"They do, mommy. There are lots of them," Lillie said. "They have guns, and they want to kill us."

Donna pushed the little girl to arm's length and looked into her eyes. "Whoever told you such a thing?"

"My friends...their thoughts told me."

"But it can't be true."

Adam heard the conversation and came onto the deck, looking at his wife as she clutched their daughter. Then he rushed to them and wrapped his arms around them both.

Donna pressed her face into her husband's chest and let his arms enfold her and her little girl.

"Call Dr. K, please, Daddy," Lillie said. "She'll help us."

And suddenly, Lillie's expression changed. Her initial reaction of surprise and worry was already gone...and in its place was a look of calm purpose and resolve.

2

Sam's massive old Mercedes rumbled into the Allonzo driveway, gave a gasp, a wheeze, and settled like a sleepy elephant. K pulled her purse to her and got out of the car just as Donna came running.

Even though the two women had never touched, Donna now hugged K as though she were a fellow survivor of a long and nasty struggle. Looking on, Samuel understood exactly what was happening but felt that the battle had only begun.

"How is she?" K asked as she made her way to the house.

"Lillie seems resigned to what's happening," said Donna. "But she definitely wants to see you."

"Almost as much as we want to see her," said K.

Lillie came running from the house then. She rushed to the doctor and wrapped her arms around the woman, burying her face against K's leg.

K pulled free, knelt, and gave the little girl a hug.

"Are you okay, sweetie?"

"You know," Lillie answered.

"Yeah, she does," said Sam.

A few moments later, they were all sitting at the table on the back deck, drinking lemonade.

"How would you feel about Lillie coming and staying with us at Leland?" K asked.

Donna glanced at her husband and then let him answer.

"I don't like it," he said. "I think we can protect Lillie better here. We've got guns, and so do our neighbors. We'll keep her safe from the crazies."

Sam looked at K and then at Lillie.

"And what do you say, honey?"

"I don't like guns," she said.

"No one does," said K.

"Some people do," answered the little girl.

"They're fine in their proper place," said her father. "And they may be necessary to protect you, Lillie. You want me to protect you, right?"

"I just want to be safe."

K smiled at Sam and then turned back to Lillie.

"Leland wants to build a safe house for children like you," said K, "right on our campus. We hope to find a benefactor to provide enough money to give you a place that will be safe from the bad guys."

"Okay," answered Lillie. "But what's a benefactor?"

K shrugged. "People who give you something just because they care about you."

"And what do they want back?"

"That's the thing," said Sam. "They don't want *anything* back. They give just because they want YOU to be well."

"Always?" asked Lillie.

"A very adult question," said Sam with a knowing smile.

K thought about it before answering and then told a comforting lie. "Yes, honey...always."

"Kindness everywhere?"

"Exactly."

The little girl didn't say anything after that; she just sat there with a puzzled look. Then, finally, she added one word.

"Scary."

K waited, not knowing exactly how to respond. Finally, she said, "There will be children like you there."

"Like the ones I talk to in my head?"

"Melissa and Ángel...yes."

"And can Mommy and Daddy come?"

"I think so," said K. "We're working on that."

"Then, I'll come," said Lillie, and she smiled for the first time in three days.

EIGHTEEN—K, Samuel, & Bobbie

(Office of the Provost, Leland University)

MIDTOWN DESPERATION

Parker stared at the blank television screen. The set hadn't been turned on in at least two weeks. It was now just part of an ugly ritual: Parker, at the office, ignoring her coworkers, keeping to herself, hoping no one would notice the tears in her eyes as she did her best to concentrate on her job. Thankfully, no public contact was required.

She would drive home then, prepare some god-awful TV dinner, and sit in front of the television, trying to eat something but lucky to get down a bite or two at best. The TV was off the whole time.

Then, up to bed, alone, no dreams, not even wishful thinking about Jason. She would just lie there. Eyes closed, that awful feeling in the pit of her stomach as though some giant boulder was lodged inside of her...filling her up, holding her in place, not allowing her to move.

It was there right now as she lay sobbing...wondering how she could put her life back together again and

knowing that it was
impossible.

"How could you, Sam?" K growled from across the room.

"Easy," he answered. "What's a romance novel without the depths of despair? You must know, K. Haven't you ever been hopelessly in love?"

"No comment," she said as she strode across the outer office and handed the rumpled manuscript pages back to her boss. "But you'd better come up with something damn good before this story goes any further."

Sam stared back at K, a critical question hanging in the air between them, and then K just said it out loud.

"And what's the point anyway?"

"The point," Sam said as he took a deep breath, went to K, grasped her shoulders, and shook her lightly, "is that we have to be strong now. The kids are depending on us."

"And not be like Parker?" K said, trying for a hopeful smile that failed.

"Ángel is recovering nicely, isn't he?" Sam asked.

"According to the latest medical report."

"So, let's see what we can do to help keep him safe."

"And all the others, too," added K.

"As many as we can."

Just then, the door to the outer office swung open, and Homeland Security Special Agent Bobbie Jenkins stood in the doorway, carrying an attaché that looked as beat-up as she did.

"Fucking military transports," she grumbled as she pulled out a cigarette and stuck it between her lips."

Sam immediately waved her off. "No smokes inside the buildings."

"Of course not," bitched Bobbie. "What did I expect, some civility at the Harvard of the West?"

"It's just..." K began.

"I know what *it's just*..." said the agent as she shuffled into the room, swung herself into one of the chairs, and turned to K.

"Don't suppose there's any place handy where a tired girl can...."

"Freshen up?" suggested K.

"Take a piss."

"Out the door, turn left, down the hall, about five paces, and...."

"Clear enough, Sam," said Bobbie, and she pushed herself up from the chair and charged out of the room.

"Should I go after her," asked K. "Maybe calm her a little, make her more presentable for the provost?"

Sam laughed and just shook his head. "At your own risk," he said.

But K did it anyway.

2

Dr. Marjorie Mendoza was what her colleagues called an academic politician with a record of success going back decades. She not only knew the players and could talk the talk, but she also held the record for grants and aid coming from the widest variety of donors. So, if anyone could help K get the funding she needed for her special project, it was Marjorie.

The provost moved gracefully out from behind her desk. She wore an elegant but understated navy wool suit and a white silk blouse with a gold pendant. She held out her hand to Samuel Wentworth and gave him a welcoming grin.

"Sam," she said.

"Boss," he answered, doing his best to make his handshake as firm as hers. Then he gestured to K. "And here she is."

"Dr. Kelly," said Marjorie, moving quickly to K and giving her an equally crushing grasp.

K nodded and managed not to cry out in pain.

"And this is special agent Barbara Jenkins from the Department of Homeland Security."

"Barbara," said Marjorie as she moved toward the imposing woman.

"Bobbie, please."

They shook hands, this time Agent Jenkins getting the best of the power struggle and making the provost smile at her with new respect.

"Let's have a seat, shall we?" said Marjorie, and the four of them moved to the comfortable chairs surrounding a small conference table just to the right of her desk.

"So sorry to hear about Ángel," said Marjorie. "But he is recovering, I hear."

"Thankfully, yes," said Sam. "His little friend...Johnny wasn't so lucky...we lost him."

"Bastards. Pardon my French," said Bobbie as she reached into her attaché and pulled out her iPad. She held it up, showing the others a new website that had just appeared. Its title filled the screen.

HUMANS FOR HUMANITY.

"This is brand new as of this morning," Bobbie said. "Just another one. The department now counts over a hundred internet sites all over the world...all secretly planning to find and destroy these kids."

"Chilling," said Marjorie.

"And that doesn't count those just spewing hate," added Bobbie. "Or the rabid commentary on Facebook, Twitter, and TikTok."

"This is why we're here, boss," said Samuel. "Right now, we think the safest thing to do is just get these kids into a sheltered place, somewhere we can defend them."

"And the government thinks a university campus is the place for that?" Marjorie asked, raising an eyebrow in disbelief.

"Damn straight we do," said Bobbie.

"It's what the children and their parents prefer," said K. "We do have to think about their psychological well-being."

"I thought that was what made these kids so special," Marjorie answered. "Their psyches are equipped to handle the dangers out there."

"Come on, Boss," Sam said. "These are still *children*. No matter how well equipped they are physiologically..."

"So, you *don't* want to give them protection here at Leland, Dr. Mendoza?" asked Bobbie.

"Of course I do," she said. "Just making sure we have as many answers as we can."

"There's only one answer that counts," said Bobbie. "The crazies are out there, planning to exterminate these kids. The press has decided to vilify them for God only knows why..."

"And we need to help them. It's that simple," added K.

"Of course," said the provost. "And I think we'll be able to. I've already spoken to the board, and they agree. So, if we can find the funding, we can build a little retreat the kids...one where we can keep them safe... with the help of the federal government, of course."

"We at Homeland Security have agreed to provide agents for their defense," said Bobbie.

"Great, and there's more good news," Marjorie said. "The university has identified a plot of land across Highway 280...far enough from our main campus so that normal student life won't be compromised."

"I like that," said Bobbie.

"AND...I think we've found a donor willing to fund the entire project."

K's entire expression changed at that moment. She had been reticent... concerned... defensive. Now, her eyes sparkled the way they did when she first told Sam about her discoveries. She glanced over at Sam, who returned her look of excitement.

"Do you know the developer, Charles Hodgson Wolf?" asked Marjorie.

"Wolf Homes, Wolf Construction, Wolf Shopping Centers, Wolf Hotels," said Bobbie.

"Mr. Wolf appears to be all for this project," said the provost.

"He'll be flying here tomorrow morning. I'd like us all to meet him and assure him that this is an important investment in the future."

"Sounds good," said Bobbie. "Maybe I'll even get a chance to wash out my undies before I meet him."

Marjorie glanced over at Sam, who merely rolled his eyes and shrugged.

"All right then," said the provost. And the meeting ended.

NINETEEN— Josh Purdy
(Chopper City—Lost Mountain, Utah)

1

The men working in the enormous motorcycle repair yard looked up as a huge, black Rolls Royce rolled slowly through the gates. The limo threaded its way between choppers in various stages of disrepair until it reached the entrance to the air-conditioned offices at the back of the lot. There, the driver stepped into the heat boiling up from the concrete and walked around to the rear passenger door. He opened it, and a man in his mid-seventies, wearing a sharkskin suit, white dress shirt, yellow tie, and Gucci loafers, stepped out.

As he did, Emma Minson, only a few weeks after her wedding and her subsequent assassination of Johnny Norris, stepped out of the office and made her way to him. Her look was a little different on the job. Mr. Purdy preferred his assistants to have a hot look... to match the hot climate, he said, and so Emma found herself in a short leather skirt, a tight-fitting blouse, a loose leather vest, and cowgirl boots.

Mr. Wolf?" she asked.

The man gave her a friendly smile.

"I'm Emma Minson, Mr. Purdy's administrative assistant. He's ready for your twelve o'clock."

"I should hope so," said Wolf.

"We've taken the liberty to prepare a cold lunch for you in our air-conditioned conference room," said Emma as she led Wolf out of the heat and into the refreshingly cool offices.

"Excellent," he answered.

The men at every workstation in the yard observed the interaction. They were certainly attracted to Purdy's showy—though recently married—assistant but were equally interested in Charles Hodgson Wolf. A few of them knew that the famous industrialist and philanthropist was also a secret funder of motorcycle clubs throughout the country. All the clubs had far-right leanings and offered intense para-military training. They gave Wolf a loosely connected but well-trained militia he could call upon if he ever felt the need.

And now, as Wolf and Mrs. Minson disappeared into the building, the chauffeur returned to the limo and drove out of the yard. He had some time for himself while the industrialist made plans with Josh Purdy, the King of Chopper City, and already a strong advocate of yet another anti-species movement called HUMANITY FIRST.

2

Wolf sat across the conference room table from Purdy, Emma, and four of his lieutenants (including Donny, Emma's new husband). The old man stared silently at them... the carefully wrapped sandwiches, bowls of salads, and soft drinks, totally ignored.

"They think I'm a benefactor," Wolf said with a bitterly sarcastic smile. "They think I'm their friend and a supporter of this new kinda human.'"

Wolf pulled a neatly folded paper from his inside coat pocket, placed it open in the center of the table, and pointed to the image that filled the page. It was Al Pringle's distorted representation of Ángel Rivera.

"See that ABOMINATION," Wolf bellowed, and everyone at the table recoiled.

"My sources tell me that the government plans to set up an encampment... a safe house for these Monsters... at Leland University. You don't mind my calling them monsters, do you, Josh?"

"Course not," said Purdy. He was a ragged-looking man with a pockmarked face, bulbous nose, and saggy jowls. He dressed in a tight chambray shirt that simply couldn't contain his oversized gut... one of the buttons holding it together had already popped earlier that morning.

His voice was a deep growl. "That's what they are, aren't they?" he asked everyone at the table.

"Monsters," Emma agreed with a solemn nod. "Yes, sir. And I'm proud to have personally dropped one."

"Really?" asked Wolf with a querulous smile.

"My wife's a crack shot, sir," said Donny. "No joke."

"Well, that's wonderful, Mr. Minson," Wolf said. "Because I have to tell you, these kids *are* a damn deadly joke on all of us. That's why we feel it's our obligation to get rid of 'em. This is a life and death issue. Bigger even than the terrible threat to our democracy that we're facing in Washington these days."

Everyone at the table nodded.

"My organization is willing to fund the development of this so-called Safe House. I plan to call it SANCTUARY HARBOR. Quite a name, don't you think?

"I like the irony," said Purdy.

"Leland owns plenty of land, of course," added Wolf as he knocked his knuckles on the table to emphasize his next few points.

"But we'll pay for the building.

"As such, we'll be privy to the plans and be able to expedite the construction. This can't be some four-year development like all those other university builds. This place has to go up in months... like a new football stadium with the season on the line and thousands of rabid alumni getting pissed off about it."

"I like it," chuckled Purdy.

"And, while all this is going on, Josh," Wolf continued, "I want you to put together a cadre of men and women who are willing to die for the future of OUR species."

"I can do that," said Purdy as he reached in front of him, picked up a Styrofoam cup full of ice and coke, and swirled it around for a moment before taking too big a swallow. The drink poured over the sides of the cup, over his scruffy beard, and down his chin. He immediately wiped his face with his shirt sleeve and kept talking. "Once it's set up, you tell us how to breach it, and we'll descend on the place like the wrath of God. Right, Emma?"

"I'll be there with my 45 strapped to my thigh," she answered, "and my cowgirl boots on."

Wolf smiled at the image the young woman's comment conjured up.

"And then we'll take out every single damn one of them Kidstrocities," said Purdy.

"This is a global problem," continued Wolf, "but we have sympathetic supporters everywhere. And they're willing to go to war with these mutants.

"I guarantee, gentlemen—and lady—if you do your part, within a year, we will be rid of these hideous monsters forever."

"Amen," said Purdy, and his staff echoed the word in an eerie fashion.

"AMEN, BROTHER. AMEN."

PART THREE
THE DEATHTRAP

CHAPTER TWENTY—WOLF
(SANCTUARY HARBOR—Leland, California)

SIX MONTHS LATER
1

Charles Hodgson Wolf stepped out of the dust covered Lincoln Town Car and surveyed the new construction built on an isolated area of the Leland University campus nearly ten miles from the main quad. A small group of people were there to meet him. He gave them all a benevolent smile, but then—as though he'd forgotten something essential—he turned abruptly, reached back onto the seat, and took out a bowler hat. Wolf put it on, checked his reflection in the car's dusty window, seeing enough to feel satisfied, and turned back to the group: Provost Dr. Marjorie Mendoza, Dr.

Samuel Wentworth, Dr. K – Kathleen Kelly, and Homeland Security Special Agent Bobbie Jenkins.

"Greetings, friends," he said with a rakish bow. Then he came forward, shook hands with each of them, and smiled.

"It's so good to be here." He took a deep breath. "Good to be alive. YES! Shall we do a complete walkaround of our new *Sanctuary Harbor Complex*?"

The team nodded gleefully. Though each of them had stopped by for routine visits during the construction, this was their first chance to view the completed work together under the guidance of the man responsible for it all.

"We built the thing in less than three months," Wolf said as they stepped carefully around the rough earth still surrounding the outside of the new building. Seeing the dirt crusting on his expensive shoes, he stomped them clean once he reached the new sidewalk that had been added only two days ago. BAM – BAM – BAM.

"A man has to protect his Guccis," he joked. "Anyway, I think we set a record here for the construction of a maximum-security apartment building designed to house up to two hundred."

The building was cream-colored, with expansive, double aluminum windows installed in orderly rows on all sides. It could have been one of the hundreds of new condos springing up to accommodate the influx of tech workers to Silicon Valley in the early part of the twenty-first century: utilitarian, comfortable, and safe.

"Impressive," said Sam, and K gave the billionaire an approving nod.

"I'm sure all the latest security features are included," said Agent Jenkins.

Wolf smiled. "You've been reviewing them throughout the construction, haven't you, Ms. Jenkins?"

"Of course," said Bobbie.

"So then, you tell me."

"Wireless, cloud-based access control systems," Bobbie began, "Video monitored security gates, security doorbell cameras, and surveillance cameras over all the parking areas, garages, and service entrances, programmable door and window sensors, smoke, and carbon monoxide detectors."

"Outstanding, Special Agent," said Wolf. "Don't you think so, folks?"

"Remarkable," said Sam as he glanced at K and then gave everyone a big grin.

"Just what the doctor ordered," added Wolf as he turned to K, "Don't you think so, *Doctor*? Isn't it just what *you* ordered?"

"Better than I could have imagined," she said.

"So, let's look inside," Wolf chirped as he put his hand behind K's back and guided her toward the front of the building. The facade was modest, with no external decorations, a simple stairway, a small front entryway, glass doors, and card-key access, nothing fancy.

"After you," said Wolf as he opened the door, let the group through, and followed them inside. The hallways between the rooms featured utilitarian carpeting and inexpensive fixtures with simple hardware.

Wolf pushed open the first door he came to and led the group into a small apartment already furnished with a couch, chairs, and a television. The kitchen had essential appliances: a small refrigerator, oven, and stove.

Two bedrooms and one small bathroom were directly off the living room.

Dr. Mendoza peered into the hallway and checked out the bedrooms.

"I think poor families would give anything for housing like this," said K.

"That's the idea," said Sam. "We need to give all these kids a good reason to move here. Two bedrooms so their parents can visit long enough to get the kids settled. Then they can go home but come back when they want to and when we need them."

Dr. Mendez took a seat on the small living room sofa. "Comfy enough," she said.

"So, tell me, Dr. K," Wolf asked. "How many of these special kids are ready to move in *right now*?"

"Ninety," she answered as she took a seat on the sofa. Sam sat in an easy chair next to the window while Agent Jenkins continued to stand.

"And another hundred youngsters are standing by waiting for full clearance," added Mendoza.

"And where are they now?" asked the billionaire.

"Mostly at home with their parents," said K. "With a few exceptions, they are all under the age of fifteen."

"I've assigned agents to each of the families...to keep an eye on them and protect them from the crazies," said Bobbie. "Though public sentiment is finally starting to turn in the kids' favor."

Sam said, "More and more people are seeing through the bad press they're getting from people like Brad Dockster and are judging the kids more positively."

"Still not enough for my guys to stand down yet," added Bobbie.

"I mean, Jesus," said Sam. "What's happened to this country? Everyone's gotten so damn bloodthirsty."

Wolf laughed. "We've always been a bloodthirsty country. Don't you know that, Dr. Wentworth? The code of the West!" He took off his hat and, for a moment, put a crease in the top, trying his best to turn it into a cowboy hat.

"At heart, we're all cowboys and cowgirls, pioneers and vigilantes."

"Yeehaw," added Bobbie.

"Amen," said the billionaire. And then he became more serious. "So, are there any international members of the group, Dr. K?"

"Twenty-four kids from Canada and Mexico," she said, "We're only working in North America at the present. Many are staying with volunteer families in California."

"Well vetted by Homeland Security, of course," added Bobbie.

"Of course," said Wolf with a grin. There was a long pause, and then, as though remembering why they had all gathered, he turned and pointed to the vents in the top corners of the room. "Best air conditioning systems money can buy. We spared no expense there. Even though your Palo Alto climate is moderate compared to my home in Cleveland, I wanted these kids to be very comfortable during their stay."

"That would be maybe for a year...two at the most...until public animosity dies down and the vigilantes, as you call them, Mr. Wolf, have turned their deadly attention to something else."

"They are a changeable bunch," the billionaire added with a knowing grin. "Can't stay focused on any one thing for too long. I give them a year at most, then your kids can go back into mainstream society and do their thing... whatever that is."

"And we can turn Sanctuary Harbor into student housing."

"Wolf Hall," said the Billionaire with a grin. "My little legacy to Leland."

"And we thank you again for that," said the provost.

2

Back in his office, Sam scooted behind his computer, logged in, and began typing away...for about two sentences. Then he stopped and looked up at K, who had taken her seat in her usual chair.

"Fuck," he murmured softly.

"Writer's block?" asked K teasingly. But Sam was serious.

"Something's just not right."

"What do you mean?"

Sam stood and walked around in front of his desk. Leaning back on it, he ran his fingers through his hair. "I don't know. Something makes me nervous about this whole thing."

"Sanctuary Harbor? Don't you think Bobbie Jenkins would have picked up on it...whatever it is, or Mr. Wolf...He's sweet, actually, an amazing old man, isn't he?"

"Yeah, he is, and remember, he's only two years older than I am."

"With ten times as much money."

"Yeah, that's right, don't remind me. And *they* should have picked up on whatever it is that's bothering me...I guess."

"Can you pinpoint anything specific?" asked K as she stood and approached her boss.

"Not really."

"Maybe you're just tired," K said, seeing the haggard look on Sam's face. "How's Parker?"

Sam chuckled then. "Not sure. I know she's heartbroken, spending sleepless nights, but otherwise, you know...not much there."

"See," K said. "Writer's block. Maybe Parker needs some new man in her life or some outside force to bring her and Jason back together again."

"Hey...that's good. An accident," Sam said, pointing at K with a sudden show of interest.

"An accident can bring them back together," added K.

"Good idea, yes!" And the old man moved back to his desk and his computer.

K turned, already hearing the rattle of Sam's computer keyboard as she opened the office door and headed out.

"I think my work here is done," she said with a happy smile.

CHAPTER TWENTY-ONE— MELISSA
(SANCTUARY HARBOR—Leland, California)

1

"So cool," shouted Javon Washington as he made his way into the Sanctuary Harbor apartment assigned to his sister, Melissa.

Unlike most other units in the complex, Melissa's space had three bedrooms. It was a unique accommodation because she was the very first of the special children to join Dr. K at Leland.

"I won't be here for long," said her mother, Serena.

Melissa's twenty-nine-year-old mom had become very active in an East Palo Alto church and had, in her own words, "found herself a man." The man in question was Andrew Tompkins, a successful hardware store owner and a devout Baptist.

"Andy is just so STRONG," Serena bragged to her daughter. "He throws those fifty-pound bags of grass seed into customer cars like he's in a weight room. And he's tall, good-looking, God-fearing, and just so KIND."

In fact, Andrew Tompkins was all that and financially secure, too.

Mr. Henry Fellows, the Leland chauffeur who brought Serena to the church, had nothing but good things to say about the young man...the only apparent drawback was that he worked so many long hours.

"As soon as the dust settles," said Serena, checking the television and seeing that they had a full range of cable channels, "I know he'll ask me to marry him."

That idea was apparently the only other downside to Andy Tompkins. He was very thoughtful and took his time when it came to life-changing decisions like marriage.

"HEY! WOW! Don't you just love the place?" asked K as she breezed into the apartment and gave Melissa a hopeful smile.

"Not sure," said the girl with a look of concern.

"What do you mean, not sure?" asked her mom.

"Just look at this," and Serena immediately took Dr. K by the hand and led her into her bedroom. "Just look at this. The big closet, the mirror over the dresser, and the great big bathroom with a BATHTUB!"

"I'll be sure to tell Mr. Wolf just how grateful you are for his generosity," said K.

"Amen," added Serena. "Of course, Javon and I won't be here very long. I'm sure we'll move out as soon as my boyfriend, Andrew, asks me to marry him."

"No rush," said K. "No rush at all." Then she wandered back into the living room and studied Melissa, who sat in the corner, trying to watch television but clearly not paying attention.

"What's wrong, Lissie?" K asked.

The girl didn't answer, just turned away.

"I thought you liked it here at Leland. Change your mind? Want to go back to Rochester?"

"Course not," said the girl. "I'll be fine. I'm just feeling a little headachy."

"I see," said K with a smile. "Maybe just allergies to the new material being used in the building. That happens sometimes."

"It could be," said the girl. "Not sure. Just feeling dizzy, worried about it, you know."

K smiled. "Come here, honey."

Melissa stood and let K give her a hug. Her response was still unenthusiastic. No hug back.

"You really aren't feeling well, are you?" K asked. "Maybe it's just a response to all these changes and the new kids."

"Yeah, that must be it," sighed Melissa.

But of course, none of them knew that a deadly clock was ticking, and the countdown to the extermination of what the press called the Monstrosities had already begun.

2

"Something just doesn't feel right about this place," said Hank Fellows as he checked out the sports center located on the main floor of Sanctuary Harbor.

"I mean, it's nice, don't get me wrong. But why is the *only* basketball court *inside* the building instead of outside?"

Javon didn't answer. Just dribbled once and took a shot from beyond the arch.

"And tell me," Hank continued, "now that all the construction equipment is out of here— why are the roads so narrow, and the parking spaces so limited? Almost feels like they're trying to trap y'all in here."

"THREE POINTS!" Javon shouted in response as he retrieved the ball, dribbled to the top of the key, and took a quick jump shot. "Feels pretty great to me."

"Swish!"

"Look at the locks on the doors," Hank continued. "All one way…. the wrong way. It's like it's easy to get in, but it could be damn hard to get out. That's just backwards."

"I don't know what you're talking about," said Javon as he dribbled up to the older man and stood facing him, continuing to bounce the ball with his left hand while he looked him in the eye.

"The stairways between the floors seem awfully narrow."

"Hank," Javon finally said. "This place is a friggin' miracle. And it's free. And it went up overnight. I'm sure they may have had to cut a few corners to get it done so quickly… but they'll make it right eventually. I promise."

"You promise?"

Javon nodded.

"Like you have anything to say about it."

"Me?" said Hank. "I'm not so sure…not with all those newspapers and websites calling your sister and kids like her MONSTROSITIES."

"You can talk to Dr. K or my mom about it," suggested Javon.

Hank sighed. "Your mom is so love-struck that she doesn't know where she is...and K...same thing...only she just loves havin' this place for y'all."

Javon shrugged, turned, and launched a half-court shot that went way wide of the basket.

"Airball!" he called. And then turned back to Hank.

"Well, there is Dr. Wentworth," he said... "Or even that nasty woman from Homeland Security."

"Yes," Hank nodded with a sudden smile. "Homeland Security? I like that idea, boy. Good thinking."

"DOPE!" said Javon as he turned and darted back across the court to retrieve the basketball.

CHAPTER TWENTY-TWO— ÁNGEL

(SANCTUARY HARBOR—Leland, California)

1

An hour later, K walked into the two-bedroom apartment assigned to Ángel Rivera.

"So, what do you think?" she asked the boy who had recovered from a gunshot wound only six months earlier. His best friend, Johnny Norris, had not been so lucky.

"It's nice," he answered without much enthusiasm. "Wish Johnny was here, though."

Ángel had just poured himself a glass of orange juice and now set both the bottle and the glass onto the kitchen counter. He tried for a welcoming smile, but the sense of loss was still in his eyes.

Apparently, K thought, members of this new species grieve in much the same way she and the rest of their predecessors do—no evolutionary leap there.

Ángel's grandfather, Antonio Rivera, walked in from the other room. He nodded to K and reached for his grandson, reassuringly pressing his hand against the boy's back.

"Johnny would have liked the place, Ángel," he said. "Maybe he can see it through our eyes. We can keep him with us that way."

"Yeah."

"And Talley Antone is down on the next floor with four more of your friends from the reservation," added K.

"I know," said Ángel.

"Want to go down and welcome them? I can go with you."

"In a minute," Ángel told K, and he took his OJ, walked into the living room, and sat on the couch.

Finally, after a long silence, he turned to his grandfather. "Not quite the Southwestern Look we're used to, is it, Papa."

"Actually, a change in decor might be nice," said the old man.

"You'll be staying with Ángel for a few days then?" asked K.

"Not for long. There's too much to do at the ranch. But yes, for about a week. I brought my art supplies and thought I'd do a landscape for him... something that reminds him of home."

"Sabino Canyon, one of my favorite places," suggested Ángel, finally giving his grandfather an encouraging smile.

"Funny thing," said Antonio, pulling out his iPhone and turning it toward the boy. "I managed to download a few dozen pix of the place. You should be able to find the perfect scene in there somewhere."

Ángel seemed touched by his grandfather's generosity. Tears formed in his eyes, and suddenly, he doubled over in grief. K began to move toward him, but Antonio held up his hand and stopped her.

"He's okay, aren't you, son?"

Ángel stayed hunched over, sobbing for a long moment, but then he gathered himself, straightened up, and wiped the tears from his eyes.

"Yeah. This has happened to me before," he said. "When I start having any kind of serious feelings, I start to cry. Sorry."

"We understand," said K.

Antonio nodded.

"I'm fine now," said Ángel. "Let's go down and see Talley."

2

Talley Antone was on the second floor of the complex. Like most other rooms on the floor, it was a studio apartment with a small kitchen area opening on a living room with a sofa bed. Talley had folded the bed back into a couch, and three of her friends from the reservation—all members of the new species—were sitting there when Ángel, Antonio, and K arrived.

"Seems just right for me," said Talley when asked how she liked SANCTUARY HARBOR. But then there was a long pause, and she added, "I mean, not sure, actually."

"How come?" K asked.

"I don't know...there's a scary feeling here."

K went to the small chair in the corner and sat down. Her expression turned to one of concern.

"You know, I really don't know how to cook, but Auntie Edna is here, and she's going to stay for a month."

Edna turned from the corner of the kitchen where she was preparing sandwiches and nodded to the others.

"Want something to eat, Ángel?" she asked.

"No...I'm good."

"How about your friends?"

"What ya got?" asked Antonio.

"Right now, bologna sandwiches and potato salad," said Edna.

"Sounds great." said Antonio, "I'll take two."

"And you, Miss?" asked the woman, turning toward K.

"Maybe just a little potato salad."

"It's good bologna. I brought it from the rez."

"Okay…what the hell…time to celebrate, right?"

"Bologna celebration?" she said to Talley, but the girl still kept that troubled expression.

The two stared at each other for a long moment. Maybe Sam was onto something, she thought. But then Auntie Edna spoke up. "That brings up an interesting question, you know. Just how do you propose feeding all these kids?"

"There's a dining hall on the first floor," said K. "It will serve three meals a day."

"Including breakfast?" asked Hector Bigay, one of the boys from the rez.

"Absolutely," answered K, "And a variety of soups and sandwiches for lunch."

"Then why the kitchenettes in the rooms?" asked Edna.

K took a big bite of Edna's sandwich... an American classic: bologna and mustard on white bread.

"Oh, that's so good," she said, pointing to the sandwich. "Reminds me of being a kid. Anyway, I think someday they hope to convert the place into condos for high-tech workers."

"Too bad we can't transport it back to the rez," said Edna. "We could use this kind of place, don't you think, kids?"

The four Indian boys, sitting on the couch devouring their bologna sandwiches, ranged in age from six to twelve years old. Each gave a positive nod.

"My mom and dad would love it," said Hector.

Six-year-old Billy Redwing offered a simple thumbs up and a broad, sandwich-filled smile.

"I think you'll be happy here, kids," said K, "at least until the dust settles, and we can move you back into the real world again."

"And when will that be?" asked Hector.

"We're hoping within two years," said K, "but it all depends on public opinion."

"You mean the opinion that we're monstrosities?" asked Hector as he rolled his eyes.

"Well, actually, Talley IS a monster," said one of his friends.

"Not as much as you are," the girl countered as she finally snapped out of her reverie.

"I've seen what happens to you at midnight, Talley."

"And what's that?"

"I think she turns into a werewolf," said Ángel with a grin. And suddenly, everyone turned to stare at the boy. It was the first joke he had made since his friend, Johnny, was murdered.

CHAPTER-TWENTY-THREE—
LILLIE
(SANCTUARY HARBOR – Leland, California)

1

A short time later, K visited the apartment assigned to little Lillie Allonzo and her family. It featured a main bedroom with a king-sized bed for her parents and a small kid's room with a giant rainbow painted on the wall. That's where she found Lillie.

"And how do you like the place," asked K.

"It's nice," Lillie said as she gestured to the bunk beds in the corner. "Maybe someone can visit and spend the night."

"Maybe," answered K, a little distracted by the fact that Lillie seemed less than enthusiastic.

But then the little girl turned quickly and gestured to the corner of the room. "I have my own desk. I like that."

The tidy white desk fit neatly into the corner, and a brand-new iPad was sitting in its center.

"Mister Wolf spared no expense," said Donna Allonzo.

"He's just been so generous," K added, and then she looked over at Lillie's father, who had just walked into the bedroom. "What do you think, Mr. Allonzo?"

"Perfect for me...for all of us," he answered. "Donna can stay with Lillie for the next few months, and I'll be able to drive down and spend the weekends."

K and the little family walked back into the living room. Although the place was meant to house a single little girl, it was a large apartment with a kitchen, a living room with a big-screen TV, and a bathroom with a tub.

"This place could go for over four-thousand a month," said Adam. "What was this guy Wolf thinking?"

"Future re-use, I'm sure," said K.

"Smart guy," said Adam touching his fingertip to his forehead. "Brainy...no wonder he's so rich."

"But are there other children for Lillie to play with?" asked Donna as everyone took a seat in the living room.

"Absolutely," answered K.

"And preschool?"

"Leland is a little worried about sending the kids to the local schools," said K.

"Bet they fear the monster hunters will be after them," said Adam, "endangering even the local kids?"

"Exactly," answered K. "That's why we've arranged to have some of Leland's education majors to student-teach right here in this building. Counting new species-kids from other countries, there are about fifteen boys and girls of preschool age. So, Lillie will have a chance to make lots of new friends."

"Perfect," said Donna. "Don't you think so, Lillie?"

"I'm scared, Mommy," said Lillie as she climbed onto her mother's lap.

"But why, baby?"

Lillie rubbed her little fists into her eyes. "I don't know, I just am."

Donna turned to K with a look of concern. And the doctor felt compelled to say something. "There's a little bit of scariness associated with being in a new place. I've seen it in several of the kids," she answered.

"You'll be okay, baby," Donna said, kissing the little girl's forehead. But in response, Lillie started sucking her thumb—something she hadn't done in years.

Meanwhile, Adam sighed, walked to the fridge, and pulled out a frosty can of Coke. "Well, *I love here,* anyway," he said. "It's almost too good to be true. Don't you think so, Dr. K?"

"Actually, yes," said K, feeling a bit of a chill as she watched little Lillie. "It *is* almost too good to be true."

CHAPTER TWENTY-FOUR— SAM
(HIS OFFICE—Leland, California)

1

"So, what exactly worries you, Sam?" K asked. She paced back and forth across her boss's office, her arms folded tight across her chest, her own brows furrowed with concern.

"Not sure," the old man answered. He sat behind his desk, well into the new chapter of Parker's Tragic Romance.

"Something just doesn't add up," he said. "A basic building with chintzy carpeting and fixtures, but the best air conditioning system in the world. In a place that rarely needs AC."

"Maybe Wolf is concerned about global warming," said K with a forced smile. "I mean, he builds condos and shopping centers all over North America. Maybe he's privy to some information that hasn't reached the rest of us."

"Maybe," answered Samuel. "Or maybe he's a monster secretly planning to join forces with Brad Dockster and exterminate the kids."

"Don't say that!" K said as she studied her old friend and wondered if he could be right.

"Nah," answered Sam at last. "He's too well vetted by the university; The provost has worked with him for years. And Bobbie Jenkins is a nationally known security expert, and she and Wolf are as thick as thieves. They practically sleep together."

K grinned. "There's a chilling thought."

"Sleeping with old man Wolf or with Bobbie?"

K laughed. "Either one."

"Your choice, not mine," said Sam. "Anyway..." and he took off his glasses, squeezed the bridge of his nose as if he could get rid of the growing headache that way, and then put them back on.

"I'm going home. Gotta be ready for Wolf's Press Conference and Grand Opening tomorrow."

"Oh, right. Jesus," said K, eyes suddenly wide with alarm. "I almost forgot."

"Better not," Sam answered. "Meet you back here at 9:30 AM, and we can drive to Sanctuary Harbor together. We can sleep in till then."

"Not sure I'll be able to sleep."

Samuel gave his friend an understanding smile. "Come on, K. Don't worry. In fact— and his eyes suddenly lit up— "if you want something to take your mind off all the negative thoughts...there's this." And he grabbed a printout of his latest chapter and handed it to her.

"Oh God, not now."

"Yes," said Sam as he pushed the papers into K's hands and walked slowly toward the door. "Feel free to stay and read it here if you want."

"K nodded; she had already sunk back into the comfortable chair.

"And don't bother to lock up," Sam continued, "Kaitlin will be here to do her nightly proofreading. She can shut the place down."

"Right."

2

MIDTOWN DESPERATION

Parker strode through the pouring rain, heading to work, not in the mood to spend another day at the office and definitely not looking where she was going. Ahead of her, an anxious crowd stopped abruptly, waiting for the light to change so they could march on. But instead, as traffic surged through the intersection, splashing the crowd with high waves of rainwater, they backed up, forcing Parker and those behind them to stop under an awning sagging dangerously in the downpour.

Parker looked up at it, still heartbroken, still not giving much of a damn about her life, her unrequited love for Jason, or anything else.

Maybe returning to Duluth wasn't such a bad idea after all, she thought. There was almost certainly a job waiting for her, and—as far as Jason was concerned—what chance did she have, anyway? She should have been well over him by now. Except, of course, she wasn't.

Unable to get out from under the awning, she missed another light, would probably be late for work, and get another nasty lecture from the boss.

Still, who cared, really?

A blast of wind swirled her hair around her face, pasting it to her eyes, and jostled the workers huddled around her. And then—worst luck of all this awful morning—the awning collapsed, dumping an ocean of rain onto Parker and fifteen other struggling New Yorkers, and leaving them trapped under the heavy canvas.

Parker held her breath...

The door to Sam's office swung in as Kaitlin entered. She wore tennis shoes, a short plaid skirt, and a white cotton blouse, with a cardigan sweater tied around her neck.

"Oh, hi, Dr. K, didn't know you would be here," she said as she spotted K sitting in the easy chair reading the manuscript. And then she grinned. "Oh no. He's got you reading that stuff, too?"

"Yeah. As a friendly favor."

"And what do you think?" Kaitlin asked.

"Well, you know…not my taste, but the books sell. And who can argue with that?"

"So true," said Kaitlin. "Personally, I think they're kind of meh. But I've been working on them for a couple of years now, so I guess I'm used to it."

"You were working here last spring?" K confirmed.

"Yeah…yes, I was."

The girl pushed a stick of gum into her mouth, walked behind the computer, and logged in.

K watched how casually she went to work and how 'at home' she seemed behind Sam's big machine.

Dr. K stood and walked slowly to the desk.

"I'm sorry, she said, "even though I know you, Kaitlin, I don't think we've been properly introduced.

"My real name is Kathleen…Kathleen Kelly," and she held out her hand.

The girl barely looked up, kept chewing her gum, but did reach out and took K's hand. "Hi," she giggled. "I'm Kaitlin…Wolf."

K held onto her hand.

"You don't happen to be related to Charles Hodgson Wolf, the man behind the new Sanctuary Harbor complex?"

Kaitlin tried to pull her hand away, but K held onto it even tighter as the girl suddenly glanced at her suspiciously. Then, after a moment, she added, "Yeah, he's my granddad. So what?"

K released Kaitlin's hand and continued to watch as the girl finished logging into the computer and then opened the folder containing the chapters of Sam's novel.

"Is the folder with my daily reports on the desktop?" K asked.

Seemingly without thinking, the girl answered, "Yeah, sure. Why?"

K waited as the girl continued to work without looking up. Then she asked, "Kaitlin, did campus security ever talk to you about the classified information that was leaked to the press?"

Again, the girl didn't even look up...just kept typing.

The streetlight just outside the office window suddenly popped on. It was already darkening on the main quad. Soon, evening would spread across the campus, and—except for those few well-placed streetlights—Leland University would be in darkness.

"Did campus security ever question you about leaking classified information on my reports?" K asked again.

"No, they didn't," said the girl. "And if they had, I would have said 'no.'"

"No?"

"No. I never shared any of your reports with anyone."

"Even though you know they're on Sam's computer."

"Are they?" Kaitlin asked, batting her eyes in feigned—but annoyed--innocence.

"You know they are," insisted K. "Now please tell me about your grandfather...all about him. What does he really think about the new species?"

Kaitlin leaned back in her chair and stared at K.

"I don't mean to be rude, Dr. K," she said. "But I've got to finish this for Dr. Wentworth, and then I've got my own studying to do. So, if you don't mind...."

K didn't move. She just stared at the girl.

Kaitlin sighed, "Okay. Well then, you know...he thinks they're great, wonderful, need protecting. He's paying billions to protect them."

K didn't say a word, just continued staring silently at the girl, who suddenly began to shake. Her fingers trembled above the keyboard. She pulled them into her lap and held them there as tears slowly spilled onto her cheeks.

K repeated her question softly. "What does your grandfather think about the new species of children?"

"Excuse me, please," said Kaitlin, suddenly jumping to her feet and running from the room.

2

An hour later, K sat with her head in her hands. Kaitlin had gone, but in her wake was K's growing certainty that the girl's grandfather—the builder of the complex K had helped fill with a new species of kids from all over the world—was planning to exterminate them. In fact, it might already be starting. Somehow Melissa and the others had known 'something *scary*'—Lillie's word—was about to happen but didn't know what.

It would be the air conditioning, of course, K realized. Sam was right. Gas through the air ducts. How fucking obvious.

If there were only some way to reach the kids, K thought. If she could get a message to them, maybe there was still something they could do at the last minute. They did have extraordinary powers.

She picked up her cell phone, called Melissa, and listened to fourteen rings until a pleasantly robotic message said,

The party you are calling is not available at this time.
Please call again when it is convenient.

K called both Angel's and Lillie's parents with the same results.

K ran to Sam's computer. Surprisingly, in her bitterness, Kaitlin hadn't logged off. Dr. K knew everyone's email address and tried to reach them individually but got the same message each time she tried.

This email address you are trying to reach is not responding.
It has been terminated and will not be available in the future.

Did this mean that the kids' parents would be gassed, too?

No, thought K, he couldn't do that. Killing the kid's parents would be an inexcusable crime. But then, what was the genocide of an entire species?

K had no idea how Wolf planned to get away with the public execution of forty-six children, but maybe he'd found some angle. After all, he was a billionaire with a whole army of lawyers backing him up.

Anyway, none of that mattered. Wolf had already cut off all communication to his death chamber.

How do you communicate with a species that knows how to talk to each other with their minds but can't do it with the rest of the human race?

Call Sam, she thought. Call Bobbie. Surely, the gal from Homeland Security would know some way to break through to the building and get the kids to safety.

K picked up her phone and dialed Bobbie Jenkins with the same damn result:

The party you are calling is not available at this time. Please call again when it is convenient.

She called Sam then, but of course, *his* phone signal was dead too... so was his email.

"I'll fucking *run* over there if I have to," K said, getting to her feet and charging to the door. It was locked. Sure, it was. University security was certainly in Wolf's pocket by now.

Sitting down, burying her face in her hands yet again, feeling her heartbeat racing out of control, K spotted something across the room...Sam's massive old computer.

She let out a loud scream and rushed to it, yanked the power cord from the wall, grabbed it, jerked the whole huge machine off the desk, and carried it to the door, where she heaved it against the lock with all the strength she had.

It bounced off the door, and the wall, barely scratching either.

"You've got to be kidding me," K sobbed as she picked up the massive machine and threw it at the door again.

NOTHING! Not even a shutter or a scratch.

"DID THEY BUILD THIS PLACE OUT OF CAST IRON!" K screamed as she staggered back to the easy chair, sat down, and tried to catch her breath, feeling increasingly desperate with each passing moment.

"Jesus," K thought, shaking her head. She closed her eyes and did something she hadn't done since she left grade school... said a prayer. And then—thinking it might be the best behavior model for what she needed to do next— K tried to use her mind to give the kids in Sanctuary Harbor a warning. She sent a prayer of a message...not to any saint or any god, but to the members of the new species, hoping that somehow one of them would hear her.

K knew *she* wasn't capable of mental communication. But what the hell else was there to do?

3

"K."

"Dr. K?"

"Kathleen?

"DOCTOR KELLY!"

K felt someone holding her arm and shaking her. And suddenly, she woke up... looking into the concerned eyes of Doctor Samuel Wentworth.

Then she gasped. Because, behind him, she could make out the smiling face of.... "

"NO!" she called.

YES!! KAITLIN WOLF!

K took a deep breath, held it in, then slowly exhaled. She barely felt alive. Her body ached all over, and that's when she realized she'd been there all night...in Sam's office...in that now not-so-easy chair, and...

"WHAT'S THAT BITCH DOING HERE?" she screamed.

"Which... bitch... who?" Sam responded in shock, and then he just smiled.

"It's just Kat...Kaitlin."

"Kat? She's Kat to you? And did you know she's the daughter of that billionaire monster who has probably ALREADY EXECUTED the kids from the new species?" K blurted out.

"She told her grandfather all about them... she admitted it last night, and..."

"What?" Kaitlin rolled her eyes and laughed. "I don't know what you're talking about, Dr. K. We hardly spoke to each other last night."

K looked at Sam, who shrugged. "It must have been a dream," he said.

"No! Sam, I swear, I was locked in this room...no phone access to anyone. I tried to call you, I tried to call everyone, but I got no signal...it was like everything around me was shut down. I tried e-mail...no connection. So, I grabbed your big, old computer, lugged it over to the door, and tried to break out."

Sam pointed to the computer now sitting on his desk. "Did you put it back after you threw it at the door, K?"

K glanced at her old boss, then at the girl who only smiled at her curiously.

"No. I didn't, but...."

Sam pulled out his phone and checked it. "No calls from you, K."

"I told you I couldn't get through."

"You were dreaming," Kaitlin said.

Sam thought for a moment. "The door wasn't locked when we came in here."

He thought a little longer. "It certainly seems like you just had a bad dream."

K tried to collect herself. Was that possible? She stared at Kaitlin, who smiled, seeming to be the innocent young woman K always thought she was.

"Grand Opening starts in an hour," the girl said.

"That's it," K suddenly shouted. "Wolf was going to execute them all last night...all the 'new species' kids."

Now Sam's expression had become indulgent.

"I stopped by this morning to check on the setup for the demo," he began. "Bobbie Jenkins has the place crawling with special agents inside and out."

"Still..." K started. But Sam held up his hand to silence her. "I talked to Bobbie, and she told me the kids were all up, looking forward to the day, seeming more optimistic than ever."

"Optimistic," not a word she'd usually associate with the new species... but all right. K felt like this conversation was more of a dream than all of last night.

Kaitlin stepped forward then. "Ceremony starts in an hour, Dr. Wentworth."

"Great," he answered, then he turned back to K. "Just enough time to freshen up. If you want to."

K's head was reeling. Calm, she told herself. Be calm.

"I want to come," she said.

"Good," Sam answered, as he pulled her aside and whispered, "Look, I've had my concerns too, but right now, it looks like everything is under control. I think we're going to be all right...at least for this morning. So, get you back to your place, get you all scrubbed and polished, get some coffee into you, and we can still make it to the opening in time."

"Calm," K told herself again. *"Be calm. Musta been a dream. Had to be."*

CHAPTER TWENTY-FIVE – GRAND OPENING
(SANCTUARY HARBOR, Leland, California)

1

K had taken a shower, put on her most professional-looking suit, accepted a monstrous mug of coffee from the university coffee shop, and now she joined Kaitlin and Sam for the ride over to the grand opening. It was raining again, another unexpected storm, which—in K's mind at least—seemed especially appropriate for an event she still had such misgivings about.

The University had erected an enormous stage complete with a gigantic TV monitor, a podium, twelve chairs for the various speakers, and audience seating for nearly two hundred. That morning, workers also placed a large plastic canopy over the area, offering reasonable protection from the rain.

Homeland Security agents tried to look inconspicuous as they filled the last row of audience chairs or stood at the head of every aisle, often right next to campus police, who seemed unexpectedly glad that they were there.

When K, Sam, and Kaitlin arrived, a police officer took the girl by the arm and escorted her to a spot at the front of the audience while K and Sam made their way onto the stage and took their positions beside Bobbie Jenkins and Niles Porter.

"Looks like your people are everywhere," Sam said to Bobbie.

"We need to be here in force," she answered. "The president himself told me that he doesn't want any of these kids to get hurt in any way...at least not on our watch."

"I'm glad you're with us," added K, and the big woman gave her a surprised smile. "Nice to hear you say that, Doc," Bobbie answered. "But you wouldn't happen to have a cigarette, a cigar, or even a little PCP with you?"

K laughed for the first time that morning. "Afraid not."

"Always checking," Bobbie chuckled. "But if you had said 'yes,' I might have had to arrest you."

K laughed again, finally starting to feel like last night's trauma was a dream, and things might turn out all right.

"Time to get this show on the road," Sam muttered to himself, and—as if on cue—Provost Dr. Marjorie Mendoza moved up through the audience and onto the stage. She went to the podium, adjusted the microphone, and began.

"Friends. We're here to celebrate a major breakthrough in the protection and ultimate safety of a group that Leland's own Dr. Kathleen Kelly has identified as the next stage in human evolution."

K felt almost embarrassed by the mention of her name and the brief cheer that followed. Still, she stood and acknowledged the crowd.

"Misguided members of our own kind have endangered the safety of these special children," Mendoza continued. "Fueled by the greed and shortsightedness of some mainstream media, it suggests just how badly we need the evolutionary leap these children represent."

"HERE, HERE," shouted an enthusiastic academic in the crowd.

"Fortunately," Dr. Mendoza continued, "there are more positive thinkers among us, more noble citizens of our world who are willing to sacrifice for everyone's good. In this case, I'm speaking of none other than that well-known philanthropist and industrialist, the donor of this building and the supporter of so many critical projects at this and other universities, Mr. Charles Hodgson Wolf."

There was a sold round of applause, whistles, and cheers at the mention of Wolf's name.

"Even though he's well known as a highly successful and respected construction magnate, Mr. Wolf is almost better known for his philanthropy... for funding the Wolf Center of the Performing Arts here at Leland and for making similar endowments at universities nationwide. It's remarkable that—in a world filled with political confusion and conflict—such a man can maintain his focus on learning."

"God bless him!" shouted a woman in the audience.

"And so," Dr. Mendoza concluded, "it gives me great pleasure to introduce the head of Wolf Enterprises and the sponsor of SANCTUARY HARBOR—this species-saving building you see behind me—MISTER CHARLES HODGSON WOLF!"

Surprisingly agile for a man of almost eighty years, Wolf *ran* onto the stage, raising his arms in victory and nodding to his granddaughter. Then, hardly seeming out of breath at all, he went to the podium and gave the crowd a charming smile.

"My friends," he said. "You and I are all here on serious business... business I'm sure you will all support, if not right now, then certainly...IN TIME."

Those last two words sent a chill through K's heart, but she shook it off. No time for paranoia now, she told herself. And, squaring her shoulders, she braced herself for what was coming.

"I've often found myself in unpopular positions before," Wolf continued. "Positions that my business colleagues have questioned and later had to admit were—as the kids like to say—RIGHT ON!

"So too, my political and social efforts, as exemplified by the building you see behind me, have been talked about and judged by everyone, including yourselves.

"I really don't care what people think. I follow my instincts and what I believe is correct. And what I'm about to do on this rainy morning is something that I am certain is in the best interests of all HUMANITY!"

"What a minute. What's HE doing here?" Sam suddenly shouted as he got to his feet and rushed to the corner of the stage.

Wolf stopped momentarily and turned to watch as Bobbie Jenkins and Niles Power ran to the old professor.

"Who is it, Sam?"

"That goddamn Brad Dockster," Sam mumbled. "I recognize the murderous fuck from his editorial pictures."

"Probably just here to cover the story," said Niles, taking Sam by the arm and forcibly leading him back to his seat.

"People are sure jumpy, aren't they?" joked Wolf as he watched. And then he added, "Don't worry, Sam. It's okay. These proceedings will have a happy ending. Just like one of your romance novels."

"Fuck," the old man whispered to K. "No one is supposed to know I write that stuff."

But now Wolf was speaking again. "Believe me, cooler heads are about to prevail, folks," he said as he held up his hands to calm the crowd.

"You okay now, Sam?" asked Wolf cheerily. "K? Okay?"

Sam growled. But K did her best to smile.

"We're good here," said Bobbie.

"Thanks, Agent Jenkins," said Wolf. "She's one of the folks from Homeland Security," he told the audience. "She's here—I assume—to ensure everyone IS *secure*." He laughed, and so did the crowd.

"Okay. Good. Then," Wolf continued, "let me COMPLETE my inauguration of this vital project by introducing a man you all know by his voice alone, and I hope someday, you'll all come to revere.

"HERE HE IS." And, with those words, Wolf pointed directly at Brad Dockster, who rose from the audience and made his way onto the stage.

Wolf slapped him on the back, shook his hand, and moved away from the podium.

'Good Lord!" called Sam as he tried to force his way to his feet, but Niles Power held him fast. "Cool it, Sam," said the agent. And so the old man suddenly looked over at K and gave her a terrified look.

2

Dockster fumbled with the microphone for a few moments, then, turning to the audience, he shouted:

"Time for another edition of <u>THAT'S WHAT I THINK</u> from your friend, Brad Dockster, who ALWAYS tells it like it is."

There was an audible moan from the crowd as everyone finally realized who was about to speak. Several spectators began to boo, but their response was quickly drowned out by calls for silence from the rest of the crowd.

"TODAY'S TOPIC, FRIENDS," said Dockster,
"A STATEMENT MUST BE MADE!"

"That's right, friends, we are gathered to tell the world something they may not want to hear. But we are honest enough to say it anyway...."

Suddenly, two large banners descended from the arch above the speakers' platform and hung on either side of the stage. They were wide, colored a dark blue-violet, and emblazoned with the words:

HUMANITY FIRST

Sam was on his feet again, raising his fist, shouting, "Get out of here, you fucking moron."

K looked at her boss with terror in her eyes. Bobbie got to her feet and pointed at her lieutenant in the audience. He was about to lead his troops onto the stage when there was a massive rumble from the back of the crowd, and Josh Perdy, on his monstrous Harley hog—followed by scores of additional motorcyclists— roared into the area, taking up positions at the head of every aisle in the audience.

The riders were primarily old, grizzled men and women, but Donny and Emma Minson led a strong young contingent, all wearing t-shirts with the words 'HUMANITY FIRST' emblazoned on them in dayglow orange.

Homeland Security forces moved to confront or at least contain them, and a standoff ensued... grizzled bikers revving their engines as they faced black-suited federal security officers with their guns drawn.

After a moment, the bikers quieted their engines, and there was silence.

"That's better," said Dockster as he surveyed the scene with a nasty smile.

> *So now, let me repeat, my friends. A STATEMENT MUST BE MADE. We are here to keep our humanity pure.*
>
> *This is what OUR HUMAN SPECIES is all about, isn't it? We care for our own and ensure our house is safe, well-protected...not divided.*

'A HOUSE DIVIDED
AGAINST ITSELF WILL NOT
STAND!' REMEMBER? So let
us all stand together and
state that HUMANITY will not
be taken down by these
EVOLUTIONARY
MONSTROSITIES."

Sam was on his feet again, screaming, "YOU DON'T KNOW SHIT ABOUT HUMANITY, YOU BOZO!"

And he rushed toward the podium. But several members of the Homeland Security forces caught him and held him back.

Everything seemed to stop then and begin moving in slow motion as all the Homeland Security forces, the campus police, and even the cyclists turned to Bobbie Jenkins.

The big woman glanced around and saw beyond the faculty and friends to the members of the press— cameras rolling, shutters clicking—the cyclists revving

319

their engines at the top of each aisle while others raced around doing wheelies in the lot behind the crowd.

She saw her security forces facing the bikers, ready to start shooting. She saw Sam fighting to free himself and charge the stage, K getting to her feet with a look of terror in her eyes. But most of all, she saw Charles Hodgson Wolf standing in the corner, arms crossed over his chest, eyes boring into her, a sarcastic smirk on his face, almost daring her to let the pending violence erupt into a blood bath.

And so, she signaled that everyone should stand down. And they did, first her forces and then the bikers and the more agitated members of the crowd, letting things proceed as Dockster simply nodded and continued as though he were speaking to friends at a church picnic.

> *Think about it, gang. Do we really need an evolutionary leap? Do we need a new species to edge us into oblivion, take away our*

homes, and drive us into
extinction?
Will they help us? What
evolutionary new species
has ever helped the one it
replaced?

The roar of motorcycles and the cries of the crowd answered his question. Dockster took it all as approval and responded accordingly.

So, no matter what you
want, the truth is, we must
do what needs to be done
for our own good and that
of our children and their
descendants... all of our
species?
Let's get rid of these
monsters once and for all!

And suddenly, he raised a big, yellow, plastic, almost comical-looking remote control and held it dramatically in the air.

"GOD NO!" shouted K as her memories of last night came flooding back to her. "IT WAS ALL REAL!"

But by then, Dockster had already pressed the central button on the control panel with a flourish, and at that moment, a siren began wailing inside SANCTUARY HARBOR.

> **Relax, folks. We're just cleaning the air in there. No cause for alarm. We're filling the rooms with good old carbon monoxide...detoxing the place, as it were. It's all part of an effort to rid the planet of these Kidstrocities.**

As the siren continued to scream, some of the crowd broke for the podium. Still, more members of Bobbie's Homeland Security forces came pouring into the area, rushing onto the stage, forming a cordon around everyone there even though their boss and those beside her were now shaking their fists and railing angrily against the actions of their supposed benefactor.

CHAPTER TWENTY-SIX— WOLF
(SANCTUARY HARBOR Leland, California)

1

"WHERE THE FUCK ARE THEY!?!" screamed Wolf as he studied the enormous TV monitor at the back of the stage. It looked like the central control panel of a vast office security system, where images of each room in SANCTUARY HARBOR rotated through, a dozen at a time.

Individual cameras panned the space, and K recognized Melissa's room from some of the clothes the little girl's brother had left behind.

Sam realized that the camera set-ups must have been extensive because there were even low-angle views that checked under the beds to see if any child—

maybe in the throes of deadly gas inhalation—had crawled there to die.

"No one in the closets," noted K. "No one at the toilet retching her guts out as the result of carbon monoxide poisoning."

"WHERE THE FUCK ARE THEY?" screamed Wolf again, and at that moment, Brad Dockster suddenly shouted, "THERE THEY ARE!!" And all eyes turned toward him and then to the image he was pointing at.

Dockster touched a button on the control panel, and that one image filled the entire screen: the Sanctuary Harbor basketball court, where dozens of new-species children lay sprawled on the floor.

"YES!" announced Dockster triumphantly. "DEAD!!"

"Of course they are," said Wolf. "Do you see anyone breathing?"

The image on the screen now became a series of tight shots, closing in on the faces of one special child after another, coming so close it could detect their breath. NOTHING!

"NO!!" screamed K and nearly everyone in the audience.

Meanwhile, Kaitlin and the young woman beside her were carefully escorted onto the stage by four massive men dressed like members of Bobbie's homeland security force, though they almost certainly were not. One of the men carried a baby for the woman. Of course, no one recognized Debbie Dockster as she climbed the stairs and moved beside her husband. She looked at him with a mix of admiration and horror, almost the same expression Kaitlin now gave her grandfather.

K witnessed all of this and couldn't help but realize that last night was all real. And she wished again that it hadn't been.

Dockster, who still held the microphone in his hand, now passed it to Charles Wolf, who raised it to his lips and called, "Someday you'll all thank me for this," and then he flipped off the mic and tossed it away. It fell into the middle of the stage floor where Bobbie Jenkins ran to it, picked it up, turned it on, and shouted, "ARREST THOSE MEN. THEY'RE GODDAMN MURDERERS!"

But by then, Josh Perdy and his forces had closed in around Wolf and Dockster and the women and had blocked everyone else's view.

"SOMEONE SHOOT THE BASTARD," Sam called almost hysterically. But it was too late. As the crowd surrounding Wolf and his companions slowly cleared, Sam could tell that the old man and his entourage were gone...without a trace.

"Wolf must have known this was coming," K whispered, "and planned for it, just as he planned for everything else."

Homeland Security forces now filled the stage, many falling onto their knees, pounding the floor, looking for some secret door through which Wolf and his party could have escaped. Several members of Bobbie's force even rushed into the surrounding woods, thinking that

Wolf, Dockster, and company had somehow found a way through the crowd and out of the complex.

K thought it all looked like some crazy free-for-all, some insane sporting event until she suddenly glanced back at the TV monitor and gasped.

"OHMYGOD!"

The screen had split into four images now: a long shot of the entire gym, pictures of the immediate foreground where most of the kids lay dead, and two close-up shots that continued to switch between the tragic faces of the children—first, a shot of Ángel, then Melissa, and then Lillie clutching Mr. Rumple, her teddy bear.

The children's parents pushed their way onto the stage. Security forces—who could have blocked them—turned toward Bobbie Jenkins, but she gave them a quick nod, and the guards let the parents through.

K watched Donna Allonzo and the others move toward the monitors to get a look at their children. She couldn't help thinking how cruel Wolf had been to bring these parents here so they could watch their children die.

Cruelty, K realized, was one of the marks of her species, wasn't it? From Ancient Rome to the Spanish Inquisition to slavery to the Holocaust? Perhaps this new species would be able to leave human cruelty behind...if there was ever going to be a new species.

K watched Antonio Rivera—Angel's grandfather—move toward the screen at the back of the stage, tears in his eyes... his artist's hands trembling as the camera caught a quick glimpse of Angel and Talley.

Serena Washington and her son were not far behind the old man. K wondered how such loving parents could bear this kind of sudden grief.

"I just don't know," K murmured as she shook her head and saw Serena turning toward her... tears streaming down her face.

"My baby," sighed the young woman.

K looked past Serena and then to the tear-stained face of Donna Allonzo.

Who suddenly smiled.

2

K turned quickly back to the screen and the image of
Lillie clutching her teddy bear. The little girl seemed
more asleep than dead. And then her eyelashes
fluttered.

"Oh, My God, Sam!"

Lillie's eyes opened.

"Mommie," said the little girl as she looked around
in confusion, stretched, and gradually stood, dropping
Mr. Rumple to the floor.

"What's happening?" she asked her old friend.

The bear, of course, said nothing.

Lillie started to sway awkwardly. She took a step
forward and back...almost dancing. Then she turned and
looked straight into the camera.

"My Teddy," she said, and now she *was* dancing,
swaying back and forth in a child's emulation of some
choreography she might have seen on TikTok.

"My Teddy...Mr. Bear," she repeated and kept on moving.

K looked back at the group of parents and saw their looks changing from grief to hope to joy to amazement.

Now, another figure moved behind Lillie, dark and scary...except she wasn't. Talley Antone was smiling into the camera and beginning her interpretive performance, a mix of her tribal dances and hip hop.

K felt Sam clutching her arm, and she turned to him. "How about all this?" he said, "Guess I owe you a gigantic apology."

K shook her head. "No, Sam, it's fine."

His smile was enormous now as he looked back at the kids.

"Next thing you know, they'll be rapping," he said. And almost on cue, Melissa Washington jumped to her feet and began.

K – K – Dr. K
K – K – Dr. K
She's the boss.
She's the queen.

She the one drives this machine!

"Not very good," said Sam, "but passable."

"Since when are you an aficionado of rap?" asked K.

"Needed to study it for one of my novels."

"Not sure that qualifies you as an expert."

"Hey now, baby-baby."

"Wrong millennium, Sam," K said with a teasing smile. And then she turned back to the monitor, which now offered a single full-screen shot of the entire gym floor with the children all on their feet...all dancing in their own individual ways, unique, uncoordinated, confused, but still unforgettable.

Ángel moved to the camera and stared into it, gesturing like a TikTok star.

"It was *you*, Dr. K," he called. "You warned us."

And now, Melissa came forward, "The old man hid canisters of carbon monoxide in the basement...walled them off behind lead shields so we couldn't find them. "

"We never *did* find 'em," said Talley Antone, who now stepped forward to join the two.

332

"But we eventually figured out a way to control the nozzles at the top of each canister," said Ángel. "And then it was easy. They were friendly enough... the nozzles. So, we just—you know—talked 'em into shutting down."

"We might have ended it right there," said Melissa, "but we knew Mr. Wolf was messing with you, Dr. K. We got your messages last night and knew he was lying to you, so we wanted to *prove* what he was up to."

"That's why we decided to play dead," Talley added, rolling her eyes, and smiling. "We're very good at it, as you saw...better than any of *your* species, better than *any other* species on the planet."

"If anyone doubts us, we can show you the canisters," said Ángel. "We finally found 'em all."

And now Bobbie Jenkins pushed her way up through the crowd and stood beside K. Since the children were speaking directly to K, she decided she should be able to talk back to them.

"But do you know what happened to Wolf and his party?" she asked.

Ángel smiled. "They're in the tunnel."

"There's a tunnel?"

"Oh yeah," said Melissa. "It runs from Sanctuary Harbor all the way to the bay. He's got a yacht waiting for him there."

"But that's miles away."

"With all the construction, it was easy enough for Wolf to build it. He's even got a car down there."

"But don't worry," Talley added with a big smile. "He's trapped."

"He was stupid," said Ángel. "He put big doors on either end of the tunnel to keep you guys out."

"So, *we* just LOCKED THEM," added Talley. "Locked him in."

"And now he can't get out."

"You can pick him up whenever you want to. We'll unlock the doors for you," said Ángel.

"But not for them," said Lillie. "They wanted to kill us."

The little girl started to cry softly as the other children clustered around her, consoling Lillie and each other.

Sensing an appropriate time to end what had been the most terrifying morning of her life—and almost certainly everyone else's as well—the provost moved carefully back to the podium.

"Okay, everyone," she called. "Let's all return to our seats."

Then, turning to the monitor, she called, "Kids, can some of you come out here and up to the stage? Melissa, Ángel, and especially Lillie...come on out."

3

Provost Dr. Mendoza stood in the center of the stage with the three original kids and Talley beside her.

"Tell me, children," she said after a round of eager applause had finally died, "just what made you start dancing when you woke up?"

Melissa turned to her, shrugged, and answered, "JOY."

"We beat the bad guys," said Lillie."

The audience applauded once again.

"You sure did," said Dr. Mendoza. "And now, Dr. Kathleen Kelly, can you come up here, please?"

K glanced at Samuel, who nodded encouragingly. So, she stood and walked slowly up to the group.

"I think you might have something to say," said the provost.

K felt totally unprepared, yet she knew what had to be said. And so, she took the mike.

"In spite of all this happiness," she said, nodding to her kids, "there's a word that can't be forgotten at this time. I'm sure you will all agree after witnessing this morning's horrors.

"That word is BETRAYAL. Can you say it for me?"

Reluctantly, the crowd repeated the word.

"BETRAYAL."

"Yes," answered K. "BETRAYAL! As in, Mr. Wolf promised these kids sanctuary and then tried to use that sanctuary to kill them. So, he betrayed his promise, he betrayed Leland University, and he betrayed you. And why?

"Because he believed—based on no scientific knowledge whatsoever—that these children, like other emerging evolutionary species, will leave us behind.

"But he went further than that. He decided that they wanted to replace us. He and his spokesman—that unconscionable Brad Dockster— have been preaching this new species intends to destroy us. And so, he decided to kill them first. He thought it was a wise decision. But it was not. None of these kids has ever tried to hurt any of us, and the half-baked assumption that they might was hardly cause for attempted murder.

"I'm sure that Officer Jenkins and the other members of Homeland Security will certainly charge Mr. Wolf and Dockster with that crime or something even greater."

"As for the children in this new species, let me ask you, has any one of you ever experienced any threats, animosity, physical danger, or anything but charity from them?"

There was a long pause as the audience waited. And then Antonio Rivera called out, "NEVER," and others in the crowd echoed his words.

"That's right, never," said K. "And I know they are not about to turn their backs on us now. They are not indifferent. They will help us...as much as that seems to go against the evolutionary principles we see in nature.

"To quote Brad Dockster—in one broadcast I happened to hear— 'Mr. Darwin may not have been totally right about evolution.'

"Darwin believed in survival of the fittest, to be sure," said K. "But not necessarily survival of the fittest by the destruction of the weak. That may simply be a corollary later 'scientists' tacked on. But probably not. It was, more likely, something Dockster came up with just to advance his own career...almost costing these innocent children their lives."

And now K turned to the four children standing on the stage with her. "Will you abandon us as we enter the new world you bring with you?"

"No."

"Of course not."

"Why would we?" each answered.

"But we know this craziness will probably go on, kids. How will you defend yourselves?"

Melissa reached for the microphone, took it from K, and answered, "Like this."

And suddenly, she and Ángel and Talley all disappeared.

Little Lillie stood there for a long moment holding her teddy, and then she too VANISHED...and her teddy somehow vanished with her.

The crowd gasped.

"What?" murmured Bobbie.

K smiled at her as she took the mike back from a now invisible Melissa.

"Camouflage," she said. "An old trick of nature, and why not?

"We may have just witnessed the best camouflage ever seen on planet Earth."

Melissa's voice suddenly came back through the mike. "We will go away if we need to," she said. "We'll go into hiding for our own survival if some of you continue to try and murder us."

And then Ángel spoke up. "But we won't be far away. We'll be here to help you as best we can. That's our promise to you. And unlike Mr. Wolf, Mr. Dockster, and the rest of those..."

340

"BAD GUYS," Lillie suddenly added loudly, drowning out the word Angel almost used.

"We won't BETRAY that promise," Angel continued. "BETRAYAL is a word used by your species, not ours. Our brains don't have the capacity for it.

"GOODBYE."

"Goodbye, Mommy and Daddy," said Lillie's tearful voice.

There was a long silence. "Goodbye?"

"No, not that," whispered choked voices in the crowd.

"Not goodbye," sobbed Donna. "Not now."

"Not now," repeated Antonio Rivera.

And then, suddenly, all four of the children reappeared. "No, not now," they all said together. "We'll be with you for as long as we can, as long as you let us," added Melissa.

"And never EVER far away," said Ángel, "even if we have to go."

4

A stretch Lincoln Town Car glided slowly along the twelve-mile tunnel Wolf Industries had managed to construct—largely unnoticed—during the building of Sanctuary Harbor.

"There's a big, cast-iron door immediately up ahead," said Wolf from the back seat. Sitting with his favorite granddaughter, Brad and Debbie Dockster, and their baby, he felt safe and confident. The women looked concerned. But Dockster seemed energized, as though he was in the middle of a carnival ride.

"Mission accomplished," he said, unaware of the events that had transpired since they left the compound.

"Don't you want to listen to the rest of the proceedings?" asked Debbie.

"And hear people telling each other what monsters we are?" said Brad. "Hell no. I've heard enough of that already. I want to go somewhere where the sun's always shining, and no one gives a shit about the future of humanity."

"Sounds romantic," Debbie said as she passed her baby over to Kaitlin and cuddled up to her husband. Brad turned to her and kissed her on the forehead.

Kaitlin held the baby up in front of her and began making cooing noises to him. The kid giggled in response.

Wolf now tapped gently on the glass separating them from the driver. "I'm going to key-in the combination to the door at the end of this tunnel so we can get out of here," he said. "It will be open and waiting for us when we get there."

The driver nodded as he saw the portal looming ahead. It looked like the door to a gigantic bank vault.

"Not opening, boss," the driver said.

"Should, real soon," answered Wolf.

"Apparently not," called Dockster as the limo raced up in front of the door, and the driver slammed on the brakes.

Brad and Debbie lurched forward in their seats, and Kaitlin almost felt the baby flying out of her arms. She pulled him back and clutched him to her just in time.

"Christ, what next?" growled Dockster.

"No worries, there are ways around it," Wolf added. "I just need to reach the rest of my security force so they can open the door." And he began texting wildly.

"Hey, let's party in the meantime," said Debbie as she nudged her husband, who reached into the ice bucket behind the seat. "How about champagne for all?" Brad cheered. "I mean, we did get this far."

So, the group waited by the gate, drinking champagne and eating caviar and other goodies that Wolf always stored in his limousines.

Three days later...

"Getting a little tired of caviar and brie on soda crackers," mumbled Kaitlin as she popped another snack into her mouth and washed it down with a big swallow of Diet Coke. The driver was asleep. So was Brad Dockster while his wife nursed her baby with the look of a worn-out mom. A bucket of used diapers sat several yards behind the car.

Still, Debbie couldn't help but be surprised that the old man had the foresight to include a good supply of diapers for what was supposed to be a five-minute ride.

"Interesting."

She said the word out loud.

Wolf turned to her. "What was that?" He had fumbled with his phone for the past three days and accomplished nothing.

Debbie looked up...would have said something to the old man, but finally, there was something interesting to report.

"Woah," Debbie said as she watched the gigantic door at the end of the tunnel finally creak open. A massive police interceptor vehicle moved into position directly in front of them.

Bobbie Jenkins, Niles Power, and fifteen Homeland Security officers got out of the massive machine and marched toward Wolf's limo.

The old man slammed his fist into the arm of the driver, who suddenly started the engine, put the car in reverse, and began backing away from the security forces as fast as possible.

He was roaring backward down the tunnel when the piercing siren of another police interceptor blasted at them from behind him.

"Shit-fuck," called Wolf. "Stop this damn thing." And the driver slammed on his brakes just before he collided with the first of five police cars behind them.

Wolf turned forward just as the first police interceptor stopped right in front of them, pinning the limo between cop cars as Bobbie and company raced toward them.

Niles Power now began pounding on the passenger-side window.

When Wolf did nothing, he beat on it again, this time with the end of his gun.

"You're under arrest for attempted murder," said Niles as he opened his wallet and flashed his credentials.

"Attempted murder?" asked the old man.

"Afraid so," answered Bobbie Jenkins as she moved in next to Niles.

"You're damn lucky, Mr. Wolf," she added.

"Only *attempted*.

"The kids survived."

CHAPTER TWENTY-SEVEN— SAM

(HIS OFFICE—Leland, California)

1

Parker's Tragic Romance

Parker held her breath. At least fifteen others were trapped under the fallen awning whose metal frame had knocked each of them from their feet and pressed them down against the hard concrete of the New York City street.

A man, only a few feet from her, tried to lift the heavy canvas and, in the process, kicked Parker hard in the thigh.

"Hey! Watch it," she called. And she pulled her cell phone from her pocket

and turned on the flashlight. She looked into the space around her, which was no space at all. Like some deadly suffocating membrane, the awning had settled over them so entirely that they were isolated from each other.

"My arm," called an older man. "Get this thing off me; it's breaking my arm."

Parker could just make out the edge of the awning and the heavy metal frame, which must be crushing the man's arm.

"Calling 911," a woman in a distant corner of the space called. "You'd think someone out there would have seen what happened and come rushing to help us."

"Don't be stupid, lady," said a man with a heavy Brooklyn accent. "This here's New York. No one helps nobody."

Except, that was far from true because, within the next few minutes, the perimeter of the awning began to rise ever so slightly, and then light suddenly poured in through the near corner... enough for Parker to see a young boy, a teenager, maybe only fifteen or sixteen, his expression calm as he seemed to be focusing all his energy on the frame as though reasoning with it...

"Telling it to lift itself off of everyone?" Parker murmured.

And then the guy with the Brooklyn accent said, "Hey, it's one of them new species kids."

"I didn't think they were real," said the old man—much relieved that his arm was now free."

"Christ, buddy, don't you read the newspapers?" said Brooklyn.

Parker was about to agree. Unbelievable—one of evolution's angels from the new species, right there in Midtown Manhattan... saving lives. But then, two strong hands grabbed her under her arms and pulled Parker past the heavy metal frame of the awning and into the rainy New York morning. She felt herself lifted upright and turned to see the person helping her. It was Jason.

"I saw what happened, saw the goddamn awning fall, and recognized you," he said, "and then.... "Oh My God, Parker. I thought I'd lost you!" And he pulled her to him and held her tight.

Parker couldn't help thinking: As though you hadn't already lost me...as though you hadn't already sent me away.

"Stay here, please," Jason said, "We have to talk. It's crucial. Don't

move." And he led her to the edge of the building and went back to help the others just as three ambulances and a fire truck roared up.

Firefighters, EMTs, and other first responders descended on the scene and made short work of the awning, pulling it back against the building and then ministering to those trapped and injured.

"Need a paramedic," called Jason as he hurried back to Parker.

"No, I'm good. I just had to get out of there."

"Are you sure you're not hurt?"

"No," And then she gave him a crooked smile. "Just lucky, I guess."

But as she spoke, she knew it was more than luck. And in that instant, she caught a glimpse of the new species kid, a teenager with long, messy hair, jeans, and a black jacket, moving away from the scene, stuffing his hands into his pockets, and heading away to escape the publicity.

"Me too," said Jason.

"'Me too,' what?" Parker asked.

"I'm lucky, too," Jason answered as he looked into her eyes, then pulled her to him and hugged her again.

"Parker, I've been such a fool," he sighed as he held her tightly. "Would you give me another chance... just one more? I think I can explain everything."

Parker pulled away and looked into his eyes. There were tears in his...and hers. "You broke my heart."

"Please," said Jason. "Have dinner with me tonight. Let me explain. I think you'll understand if you'll just...."

Parker sighed. Those eyes were pleading, and that voice was so soft and sweet. And yes, he was there again—the man she loved, the man she planned to marry...at least in her dreams—returned to her by a kid from the new species. Did he deserve another chance?

"Sure," she whispered.

"Meet me at The Broadway Bistro...7:00 PM... PLEASE!".

"Okay," she answered. "I need to rest now, but I'll be there."

"Promise?"

Parker nodded. "Of course."

K spun on her heel and gave her boss a big grin. "That's very nice," she said. "I like it. But Including the new species in your story... that was kind of daring."

Sam shrugged. "Not really; I think it's time we pushed them into mainstream thinking and make the point that, far from being monsters, they could be our saviors."

K. sighed wistfully and smiled. Why not? "So, the novel is finished then?"

"Not quite," the old man answered. "Needs the restaurant scene."

"Does he win her back?"

"Of course," Sam Answered. "It's a romance novel. There's always a happy ending. I thought you knew that."

K sat on the edge of Sam's desk and leaned forward. "But what does he say to her?"

"You know, the usual stuff. He was distracted by a problem with his parents or siblings. OR someone was sick or dying or being a real pain in the ass, so he couldn't think about her...had to keep his mind clear. OR he was somehow so disappointed that he didn't know who to trust. Maybe he felt betrayed."

"Betrayed," said K with a sigh. "We do know all about that. Don't we?"

"Pretty much," said Sam.

"Betrayed," K repeated. And now, she looked sadly across the room. "But what do you *really* think about the new species kids?"

"They'll be fine. Bobbie had the Army Corps of Engineers run a full check on Sanctuary Harbor and said there were no more killing devices."

"That's what she called them?"

"Absolutely. And just to be sure, the kids apparently communicated telepathically with every electronic and mechanical function in the place and confirmed it."

"Good," K said as she hopped down from the desk and went over to her favorite easy chair. She sank back into it and smiled.

"Then," Sam continued, "she instituted security so tight you'd think the President of the United States was sleeping there every night. Guards all around...everywhere...for a year!"

"What a gal."

Sam smirked and nodded. "Not my type, a little abrasive, but yeah. She's very good at her job."

356

2

An Asian college student with short black hair and glasses knocked softly on Sam's office door. She wore a loose-fitting Leland sweatshirt, a short, plaid skirt over grey leggings, and carried a backpack.

K saw her through the glass and turned to Sam. "A new proofreader?"

"Why not?"

"Attractive."

"Can't hold that against her," Sam said with a grin.

"But you *have* vetted her through campus security before giving her access to your computer and all your files... right?"

"A little," Sam answered. "But I've also secured my research computer and brought in a second machine just for my novels. That's all Li Mei here will be able to use. The other machine is completely locked down and inaccessible."

"But still, Sam. Jesus! Couldn't you just *finish* the book and then send it to someone on the outside?"

The professor ignored K as he moved slowly toward the door, giving the young visitor a generous smile as he approached; then, at the last minute, he turned to K.

"Do you know how hard it is to find good proofreaders these days...not to mention editors. Li is fabulous, Dr. Kelly. She's already fixed things that Kaitlin never even noticed."

Sam opened the door and nodded to the college student.

"Li Mei," he said.

"Dr. Wentworth."

"Everything is ready for you."

"Wonderful," said Li. "Looks like you have a brand-new computer."

She moved behind his desk, slid her backpack from her shoulder, and dropped it beside the chair.

"Latest and greatest iMac," Sam said, "except with this baby... no access codes needed, no internet, no iCloud...no connections to *nothin'*!"

"Sounds great," said the young woman as she pushed her glasses up on her nose and nodded at the stack of pages on Sam's desk.

The pages suddenly flew into the air and fanned out into a display as Li looked at them. Glancing from one to the other, she nodded again, and the pages shuffled into a new order.

"Controlling objects with her mind," K said in amazement.

Sam just grinned, stuffed his hands into his pockets, and shrugged.

"You hired a woman from the new Species, didn't you?" asked K.

"Equal opportunity employer."

"How did you find one of college age?"

"There are a few kids like that around, Dr. Kelly," Sam answered. "You just need to know where to look."

At this point, Li must have felt that the pages were in the proper order because they suddenly lowered themselves onto the table beside her... like *magic*.

"I'll check in with you in about ninety minutes, Li," Sam said, taking K by the arm and leading her from the room.

But as soon as they were in the hallway, K turned to him.

"Sam...she's so efficient... doing so much with the power of her mind."

"Of course. Thank you," Sam said. "I found a Species II woman of college age and hired her as a summer intern. She's perfectly suited to proofing romance novels. Plus, she lives in a dorm here on campus. She even has a boyfriend, seems stable, and well-suited to the job.

"Now, can we be done with the subject?"

K took a deep breath, held it briefly, let it out, and nodded. "Yes. Yes, we can."

"Good. Now, you and I need to go to lunch, Dr. Kelly. As I said, I have a new project I'd like to discuss with you."

K grinned. "Does it involve Evolution's Angles?"

"Nice name for them, isn't it? Sam answered. "And now that Wolf and his fellow crazies have been locked up, things should be *safer* for everyone."

K felt a sudden chill run through her, and the feeling showed in her eyes. You mean there still might be someone out there who would want to sabotage your project?"

Sam frowned. "Didn't I say we'd be safer, K? I mean, no one who does this kind of research can ever be *totally* safe. They CAN'T lock up every crazy person in the world."

"Guess not," K murmured as she moved gracefully through the long research hallway, momentarily lost in thought. And then she added, "I'm sure the new project will be worth doing in spite of any dangers that might come with it. Right, Sam?"

The old professor nodded with a wry smile.

"Oh, it will be...Dr. Kelly. It *really* will be."

THE END.

ACKNOWLEDGMENTS

There's a mistaken belief that fiction writing is a lonely business...that writers sit *alone*, staring at their computer screens for endless days, months, and even years. The idea couldn't be farther from the truth. Writers are never alone when they write. They are with dozens of the most interesting people they can imagine, who are doing amazing things, challenging them to tell the story their way, not according to some preconceived notion. And, if the writer goes along with these characters and gives them what they want...well, things can work out wonderfully.

But some people *are* alone in this process: the wives, lovers, and friends of writers. They have to put up with someone locked in a room with his or her other friends, who stares at them empty-headedly during dinners, breakfasts, or even as they walk the beach together.

"You're so far away," they say. "You're never there."

My wife is such a person, and now that this book is finished, I can tell her: "Thank you for allowing me to tell my story and for loving me despite the time it took away from us. I LOVE YOU!"

I owe quite a debt to Jay Douglas, who advised me on so many story points, held lengthy discussions, and read and re-read my manuscripts. This book is so much better because of you, Jay. Thank you.

Thanks also to Bram Druckman, who started writing rants in response to some of the events in this story. Bram eventually evolved into Brad Dockster, a major character in the story, and some of his rants even made it into the book.

Thanks to Andrea Jepson for her letters of advice and encouragement. Also, to Derrick Christensen, a Goodreads friend who read my story as it evolved and gave me excellent advice and support.

Thank you, Gary Cardinale, for reading all my books and offering so much positive reinforcement.

Thanks, Debbie Thrush, for all those design and marketing suggestions and words of encouragement.

Thanks to Gershon Weltman, John Pesqueira, and John Caselli for their support. Thanks to my son Tony for all his help with the story and his advice on the title and cover. And finally, a big "THANK YOU" to my editors and proofreaders, Lauren Ayer and Janet Grady who did the hard work of fixing all my misspellings, awkward sentences, and ever-changing character names.

ABOUT THE AUTHOR

Nick Iuppa began his career At The MGM Animation Studios as an apprentice writer with famed Bugs Bunny/Road Runner animator Chuck Jones and children's author Dr. Seuss. He later became a staff writer for The Wonderful World of Disney. As VP Creative Director for Paramount Pictures, Nick did experimental work in interactive television and story-based simulations. Nick also served as Vice President and head of Media Services at the Bank of America and Head of the Learning Technologies Group at Apple Computer. NICK is the author of fifteen novels,

Management by Guilt (Fawcett Books 1984—a Fortune Book Club selection), and four technical books on interactive media. He lives in Northern California with his wife, Ginny. For more about Nick, visit *www.nickiuppa.com.*

Made in the USA
Monee, IL
22 November 2024

70828210R00207